BLOOD
TIES

Also by Ralph McInerny in Large Print:

Abracadaver
The Basket Case
A Cardinal Offense
Desert Sinner
Getting Away with Murder
Grave Undertakings
Judas Priest
Lying Three
Rest in Pieces
Second Vespers
Sub Rosa
Requiem for a Realtor

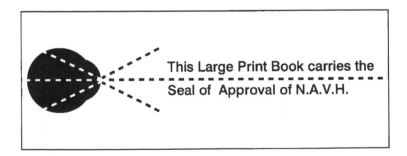

BLOOD TIES

A Father Dowling Mystery

Ralph McInerny

Thorndike Press • Waterville, Maine

Copyright © 2005 by Ralph McInerny.

Published in 2005 by arrangement with St. Martin's Press, LLC.

Thorndike Press® Large Print Basic.

The tree indicium is a trademark of Thorndike Press.

The text of this Large Print edition is unabridged.
Other aspects of the book may vary from the original edition.

Set in 16 pt. Plantin by Christina S. Huff.

Printed in the United States on permanent paper.

Library of Congress Cataloging-in-Publication Data

McInerny, Ralph M.
  Blood ties / by Ralph McInerny.
    p. cm.
  "A Father Dowling mystery."
  "Thorndike Press large print basic" — T.p. verso.
  ISBN 0-7862-7944-3 (lg. print : hc : alk. paper)
  1. Dowling, Father (Fictitious character) — Fiction.
  2. Birthfathers — Crimes against — Fiction.
  3. Birthparents — Fiction. 4. Catholics — Fiction.
  5. Illinois — Fiction. 6. Adoptees — Fiction. 7. Clergy —
Fiction. 8. Large type books. I. Title.
  PS3563.A31166B55 2005b
  813'.54—dc22   2005015191

For Tom and Bonnie Cavanaugh

National Association for Visually Handicapped
------------------------ serving the partially seeing

As the Founder/CEO of NAVH, the only national health agency solely devoted to those who, although not totally blind, have an eye disease which could lead to serious visual impairment, I am pleased to recognize Thorndike Press★ as one of the leading publishers in the large print field.

Founded in 1954 in San Francisco to prepare large print textbooks for partially seeing children, NAVH became the pioneer and standard setting agency in the preparation of large type.

Today, those publishers who meet our standards carry the prestigious "Seal of Approval" indicating high quality large print. We are delighted that Thorndike Press is one of the publishers whose titles meet these standards. We are also pleased to recognize the significant contribution Thorndike Press is making in this important and growing field.

Lorraine H. Marchi, L.H.D.
Founder/CEO
NAVH

★ Thorndike Press encompasses the following imprints: Thorndike, Wheeler, Walker and Large Print Press.

PART ONE

1

"Talk to him, Henry. He'll know what to do."

"Vivian, there isn't anything to do."

"Oh, isn't there? Then why are you brooding about it?"

"I'm not brooding."

Vivian was behind the wheel, so her remarks were addressed to the windshield, but they struck him like carom shots in billiards. Henry smiled, despite himself. Ever since a billiard table had been installed at the St. Hilary's senior center, he no longer considered their almost daily visits there just something he did for his wife. As often as not, she dragged him along to the pastor's noon Mass as well, ignoring his mild protests.

"I am not going to become a pious old man."

"Bah."

"Martin Sisk."

"You are not likely to turn into a sanctimonious ass, Henry Dolan. Besides, at our age, well, why not?"

"Insurance?"

9

"Don't be cynical."

She pulled into the parking lot behind the former parish school and parked. As she dropped the keys into her purse, she turned to him. "I mean it, Henry. Talk to Father Dowling."

"We'll see."

"And don't treat me like a child."

She was out of the car and waiting for him before he came around to help her. Viv liked to be handed out of the car, even when she drove. Gallantry had become more than a habit over the course of the fifty years of their marriage, a habit born of love. Now it was such small things that best expressed his affection for her. In recent years, their marriage had entered a new phase. They did everything together. She put her arm through his, and they started for the door. Henry hummed the wedding march, and she looked up at him, radiant. Time had not dimmed the memory of the day they had pledged their love to one another. He glanced at the church.

"The scene of the crime," he murmured.

She pressed his arm closer to her. "Think about it?"

"I'll think about it."

Inside, Viv went off to play bridge, and Henry headed for the billiard table, where

10

Martin Sisk was already chalking his cue in anticipation. Henry managed to smile. Not even Martin could spoil a game of billiards. Besides, Henry invariably beat the beaming little seventy-year-old altar boy. Martin still had the cherubic look with which he had pranced around the altar all those years ago, when they were students in St. Hilary's school, Martin the delight of the nuns. He had looked like a little priest as he scampered about the sanctuary, lighting the candles, rattling off the Latin prayers, lugging the huge missal from one side of the altar to the other. All these years later, he had offered to serve Father Dowling's Mass, but priests got along without such help nowadays. Martin had been crushed, pouting like a Fra Angelico seraph.

"You should have become a priest, Martin."

"I know!"

"Why didn't you?"

"It is the regret of my life, Henry." His voice dropped. "After Deirdre died, I talked with the bishop."

"A retarded vocation?"

"It happens all the time now." Martin carried around in his wallet a news clipping. GRANDFATHER ORDAINED. There was a photograph of the new old priest giving a first blessing to his children and grandchildren.

"What did the bishop say?"

"He laughed." Henry said this in a shocked whisper. "Then I suggested maybe a permanent deacon."

"And?"

"The man is pre–Vatican II. I should have gone to the cardinal. I think Bishop Gronski may have spoken to Father Dowling. That's why he refused me."

"Oh, I doubt that."

"You always were charitable, Henry."

Such praise from Martin was unsettling. The fact was that Henry, too, had been an altar boy, a reluctant one. In those days, when his turn came, it entailed getting up at the crack of dawn and hurrying to church, putting on a cassock and surplice and trying to keep awake during the 6:45 Mass. He had always made a point of not being teamed with Martin. He didn't want the nuns to think he might go to Quigley, the minor seminary of the archdiocese of Chicago.

"Father Dowling has an odd sense of humor," Martin said, trying to be charitable, too. Father Dowling kept the enthusiastic Martin at arm's length.

Their daughter, Sheila, and her family were the great consolation of Henry and

Vivian Dolans' life. Maurice, their son, had been a crushing disappointment until he relocated to California, where his immaturity was not a handicap. Father Dowling's handling of Martin Sisk almost seemed a reason for taking Vivian's advice and talking with the pastor about his granddaughter, Martha. His granddaughter. In his own mind, he put an asterisk before her name, as if to show that, like a recently broken record in baseball, it really didn't count. It was difficult to hope that Maurice would ever father a son to carry on the Dolan name.

Later, at the noon Mass, Henry found himself paying special attention to Father Dowling. The priest said Mass reverently but swiftly, and his five-minute homily was pithy and to the point. Witty, too, without making a show of it. Henry began to believe that he could talk to Father Dowling about his granddaughter, whose sudden interest in her birth parents threatened the tranquility of his daughter's marriage.

2

Whenever Martha Lynch thought of her twenty-two years of life, something she did more frequently nowadays, it seemed an even line that had seldom been disturbed by blips of insecurity. Was it always like that with only children? In childhood she seemed to bask in a sea of love, her mother, Sheila, almost a big sister to her, her father, less demonstrative, an inarticulate rock of stability. Yet she did not think she had been spoiled. There was discipline and order in their suburban home, and when she went off to school it was brought home to her that she must do well. Sheila had a master's in education and had taught until Martha came, but then she had decided to devote herself to a class of one. George Lynch was the premier pathologist of Fox River, Illinois.

"Most of my patients are already dead."

It was his only joke, but every time he told it he seemed to surprise himself by his levity. He left the talking to his wife. It wasn't that Sheila dominated her husband. That would have been impossible, or so it seemed. She was two heads shorter than George, and he folded her into his arms as if she were a child. Sometimes Martha thought that she had grown up like that, herself gathered into one of her father's arms, her mother in the other, the three of them against the world. Not that the world seemed a menacing place. She might have been wholly unaware of the world outside the suburbs if her parents hadn't been given to unobtrusive good works. They volunteered at the center for the homeless on weekends and took their daughter with them on Saturday mornings, when George would heap the plates high at the hot table while Sheila devoted herself to the wary children. Only later, when Martha grew critical, did she think of those Saturdays at the homeless center as visits to the zoo. The unstated lesson was plain: They had been fortunate, and they had an obligation to those life had treated differently. The great earthquake of Martha's life came when she was nine and learned that she had been adopted.

When she tried to remember it, she could never recall exactly what her parents had said, the event was so submerged in her own reaction to it. Already she had learned the reticence of her father and her mother's

15

habit of concern for others. It seemed important that she not let them know how the revelation had affected her. Once, in the car, her father and grandfather in the front seat, Martha sleepy between her mother and grandmother in back, she became drowsily aware of the adult conversation going on over her head, coded, oblique. But she knew what they were talking about. Her grandmother had asked if Martha had ever been told.

"Of course."

"And."

"It ran off her like water."

It sounded like a baptism that hadn't taken. Martha had sensed the concern in the two women, and she felt good about the fact that she had protected her mother from anxiety. Her own anxiety remained silent.

What had been her parents' secret became her own. Several times, in later years, her mother tried to talk of it, but Martha headed her off. Perhaps she was still trying to believe that she had imagined it. After all, it was incredible. How could her mother not be her real mother and her father her real father? It was like being told that the axioms in geometry might be false, parallels meet, two things equal to a third turn out unequal.

Her protection was to transform her life into a story she told only to herself.

Other kids dreamed they weren't the children of their parents — it was a cliché — but now Martha, knowing she wasn't, was free to imagine where she had come from, how her parents had acquired her, all the things she might have been if they had not adopted her. But she could not imagine a life better than the one she had. The story became one of being rescued from some terrible fate, a fate she really didn't want to know about. She might have been one of those sad little children at the homeless center who stared at her as if she were from some other planet.

Only her uncle Maurice spoke of her adopted status without embarrassment. "We're really not related, my dear. Be careful." And he had kissed her cheek again. Of course, Maurice was the black sheep who had never grown up. How could she talk about herself seriously with an older man who seemed younger than she was?

In time, Martha graduated from Barat with a degree in history and then enrolled in a course for paralegals at Roosevelt University. She had lived in an apartment near the university, feeling that she was once more visiting the world of the homeless. Like those visits, though, that time was soon over, and she was hired by Foley, Farnum, and Casey in the Loop. That was where she met Bernard Casey, the son of a senior partner. He was very bright and witty and the most attractive man she had ever seen, so attractive she could not imagine why every other woman in the firm was not in love with him. Even more surprising was his immediate and unmistakable interest in her.

"Barat?" he asked.

"And where did you go?"

"Notre Dame."

"I've heard of it."

She had told a joke. His laughter filled the room, and others turned to look. It was like a public announcement.

"I never heard him laugh before," Willa Lonum said. "No one laughs in the office." Willa was over thirty and more or less in charge of the paralegals. She had been with the firm forever, or so thought the younger women.

"Tell him a joke."

Willa did not quite laugh, but it seemed to take an effort. She needed no prompting to tell Martha all about the scion of the Casey family.

"The what?"

"Heir apparent. Prince of Wales. Golden boy."

"I suppose he's engaged."

"You suppose wrong. No one has yet passed the test."

"What test?"

"Casey senior's. Bernard is his only son."

"Are there sisters?"

Willa leaned toward her, eyes wide, and whispered, "Five. All older. They were trying for a son, and when they got him, that was that."

Martha never quizzed Willa about the Caseys; she didn't have to. Family lore poured from Willa as if she had no family of her own and lived vicariously through the families of the senior members of the firm. Willa already had the look of a maiden aunt, one of those women who devote themselves to their work and their nephews and nieces and might just as well be nuns. Willa went to Mass every morning at St. Peter's on Madison before coming to the office and was given to special devotions.

"I started a novena for you," she confided to Martha.

"It sounds like skin cream."

"Don't." Just that. Don't. Willa never made light of her religious beliefs. One morning Martha stopped by St. Peter's. Willa was in a front pew. Masses were said on the hour, and in the confessionals along

19

the side of the nave penitents came and went. Martha took a bulletin when she left. Confessions were heard all day long at St. Peter's, every day but Sunday. Most of the people Sheila had seen in the pews reminded her of the homeless center. The thought that religion was largely a comfort for the unfortunate was not one she would have expressed to Willa.

Her first date with Bernard was hardly that. They went to the Art Institute one lunch hour, impromptu. He stopped by her desk. Well, not quite. He was passing and then stopped and came back.

"Where do you have lunch?"

She opened a drawer and showed him her apple. She felt like Eve.

"That's lunch?"

"I'm on a diet."

She might have been inviting his appraisal. She got it. "I'll bet you exercise, too."

"Doesn't everyone?"

"I don't know everyone. Have you seen the Degas exhibit?"

She had seen it the previous weekend, she said. "Is that where you're going?"

"We can get some lunch there."

"I could bring my apple."

"Don't you dare."

20

They walked around the exhibit, but it was very crowded, worse than on the weekend.

"You've already seen it?"

She nodded, wishing she hadn't mentioned it.

"Then we can have lunch."

But the cafeteria in the museum was swarming with people. He turned to her.

"This wasn't a very good idea."

"Come back on Saturday."

"Is that an invitation?"

"A suggestion."

"Would you come with me?"

"Sure."

That easily, she dismissed from her mind a half promise to golf with her parents. Martha was beginning to feel that the hand of destiny was on her shoulder.

"We better go somewhere else for lunch."

"I don't have time."

"Sure you do."

"Could I tempt you with my apple?"

"You already have."

Back at her desk, he pulled up a chair and split the apple in two with his bare hands while Sheila was contemplating using her letter opener to cut it.

"One of my skills," he said, offering her half.

"I thought you didn't exercise."

"Did I say that?"

Half the fun of the coming weeks was remembering what he had said when they were together. The Saturday visit was a great success. Afterward, they had lunch in a pub and drank beer and talked, each giving the other an oral CV. At four o'clock, they were still talking.

"I'm glad you were free today."

"But I wasn't. I was supposed to golf with my parents."

"Tell me about them."

"I already have."

"All I know is that your father is a doctor and your mother . . . well, is a mother."

Suddenly she realized that they weren't really her parents. Her tales about Uncle Maurice, which had delighted him, seemed equally irrelevant. Nothing she could say of her supposed relatives explained her being in the world. Her mind seemed to fill with silence as she listened for some clue to who she really was. She felt like an impostor.

"I have to go."

"My car is nearby."

"I can walk."

"Walk?"

She told him where her apartment was.

"But that's miles away."

"I walk it every morning."

"In gym shoes?"

"Of course."

"I'll walk you there."

"No you won't." She hesitated. "You don't have gym shoes."

"I'll buy some."

They parted outside. She walked home — in street shoes, not a good idea — and then sat looking out the window toward the lake while evening enveloped the apartment in a pensive twilight. She realized she loved Bernard. He seemed to love her. So what did that mean? Someday, and soon, she would have to tell him the truth about herself. But the truth was she didn't know the truth. It was in the darkening apartment that she resolved to discover who she really was. When the phone rang, she went to it. Caller ID told her it was her mother. She did not pick up the phone. If it had been Maurice, she would have answered, but he was now in California, half a continent away.

3

At first, Sheila Lynch had thought of it as second best, making someone else's child their own, but that thought was quickly erased by the elation of being a mother. She had been devastated when she miscarried twice and then was told that she would never have a baby. Ever since she had ceased being a little girl there had been warnings about getting pregnant, from the nuns and from her mother, not that the message was ever that direct. A girl should save herself for the man she would marry. Her body was a temple to be kept immaculate until marriage, and then what had been a danger would become a beautiful opportunity. Oh, how wonderful she had felt when she first became pregnant and George was as expectant as she was. His decision to take a residency at the Mayo Clinic in pathology had sent a chill through her.

"Pathology!"

"It's lab work, mainly. I love working in a lab."

Originally he had intended to do graduate

work in chemistry, but the pull of medicine was strong. Pathology represented, in a way, the best of both worlds. The years in Rochester had been like a vacation. They lived out of town in a huge house with enough land to be a farm. They had kept horses then, and three dogs. George received an offer to stay at the clinic and teach the pathology he had learned there. It had been a very difficult decision, but he had a long talk with her father and decided instead to join a group of pathologists in Fox River.

It was in Rochester that Sheila became pregnant for the first time, but not even the resources of the famed clinic could save her baby. The next year, she became pregnant again, and after her second miscarriage she was told her fate. It was like being told she really wasn't a woman. Part of the sadness was due to her parents' obvious longing for grandchildren. Now their only hope lay with her younger brother, Maurice, and what kind of hope was that?

There had followed several very bad years. At first she refused to accept what she had been told and sent up a barrage of prayers, asking for a miracle. Wasn't every pregnancy a miracle of sorts? In the end, even God had seemed against her. She thought bitterly that she might just as well have become a nun. George had been so patient with her, in his inarticulate way, that somehow she got through the terrible despondency. But the first time he mentioned adoption she didn't speak to him for a week. She realized that she was waiting for him to bring it up again. He didn't, so she did.

"I suppose we could get a black baby easily."

"Or Chinese."

When she was a little girl, Sheila had an African-American doll, not that it was called that in those days. The thought of that doll becoming a living breathing child filled her with mixed feelings. It would have seemed like an extension of the charity work they were already involved in.

"I suppose it takes forever anyway." Adoption agencies were notoriously more demanding than God in allotting children to couples.

"Not necessarily."

One of the places they volunteered was the Women's Care Center, devoted to talking young women in trouble out of getting an abortion. The center could arrange for the Lynches to adopt one of the saved babies. Sheila agreed that they should look into it.

The girl whose baby they would have was

so beautiful it was impossible to imagine that the man who had made her pregnant would not marry her.

"That's not unusual," Irene told them. Irene managed the center, inspired to do so by an abortion she had lived to regret.

"Oh."

"Madeline could decide to keep the baby."

"A single mother?"

"It's not unheard of now. Anything is better than abortion."

"When will she decide?"

"After she meets you."

"I couldn't ask her to give up her baby!"

"Then don't. Just get to know her."

Sheila murmured, "I already know her."

"I mean really know her."

"Have you told her . . ."

"Wasn't that all right?"

Suddenly Sheila felt manipulated. All they had done was talk about the possibility of taking some baby; there had been no decision, no promise.

"It was all right," George said. Sheila was flooded with emotion. She herself desperately wanted a baby, but she wanted her own. Hadn't she realized that George, too, had lived through the months of her pregnancies with visions of fatherhood dancing in his head? Of course he had. It helped Sheila to tell herself that she was doing this for George.

Their conversation with Madeline had never touched on the reason they were having the conversation. It was an hour of chitchat, about everything in the world but the baby Madeline was carrying. How must it have been for the girl to think that the life she was carrying would be separated from her forever at birth? Sheila tried to think of Madeline as a daughter, but that was impossible. She wasn't three years older than the girl. So she imagined Madeline was her sister, to whose aid she was coming in time of trouble. What had Madeline imagined?

"Taking the baby home," Irene said. "And facing her parents with a bundle in her arms."

"Do they know?"

Irene shook her head. How was it possible for parents not to know their daughter was expecting a baby? It turned out they lived in California. Madeline was a student at Northwestern; as far as her parents knew she was dutifully going to classes. That was what Madeline told them in her letters home.

"She likes you, Sheila," Irene said. "She says you will be the mother she can't be."

Sheila burst into tears that washed away any reluctance she had to take Madeline's baby. The last time Sheila saw Madeline, she was nearing term. Sheila took her in her arms, and they sat for a long time in silence.

"Thank you," Madeline said, and began to sob.

"Thank you," Sheila said, and she, too, was crying. Two weeping women who would never see one another again.

The transfer was almost sleight-of-hand. George assisted at the birth, and the baby was taken away immediately before Madeline came out of the haze. It was brought to the waiting Sheila.

"You have a girl," the nurse said.

George came out in street clothes, and they drove away with their baby.

Fifteen-year-old Maurice, fresh from his most recent expulsion from school, was godfather at the baptism, at her parents' insistence; they thought it might help him grow up. But afterward he had taken the second cousin who was godmother out to his car, where they had been surprised in a sweaty embrace. Of course the Dolans blamed the girl. Why were others always leading Maurice astray?

4

If Marie Murkin had to pick the alpha and omega of the people who made use of the senior center Edna Hospers ran in what once had been the parish school, she wouldn't hesitate, not for a minute. It would be Martin Sisk and Dr. Henry Dolan, and Martin would be the end of the alphabet. The rectory housekeeper often lamented the liturgical revolution that had changed the Church of her not so pious youth into, well, no need to go into that, but one thing she didn't miss was altar boys. There had still been a gang of them when she came to work at St. Hilary's, fussed over by the Franciscans, little urchins transformed into miniature friars when they vested to do their duties. It had been the Fe Fi Fo Fums — as Marie had irreverently dubbed the OFMs in the privacy of her own mind — who insisted on a surplice with a cowl, as if the kids, too, were friars. Part of their training seemed to be learning how to treat the housekeeper with the same merry contempt the priests showed. Honestly, there were days when

Marie went up the back stairs to her room and looked in the mirror to see if she really was invisible. But she had toughed it out and fought the temptation to leave on a fiery note, and in the fullness of time the Franciscans left and Father Roger Dowling was made pastor, so the parish was back in the hands of a real priest. It seemed a clear case of virtue rewarded.

"What do you know of Martin Sisk, Marie?" Father Dowling had asked some weeks before.

"What's he done?"

The pastor laughed, but not like a Franciscan. "He wants to serve Mass."

"That's your department," she said, after an icy silence.

"I'm glad to hear it."

"It would be a mistake."

"Why?"

"I should tell you he spoke to me first."

"And that disqualifies him?"

Well, it had almost made Marie overlook the man's faults. She was not immune to a reminder that in a sense she had seniority over the pastor, and Martin had been what Father Dowling would have called unctuous.

"Why don't you like him, Marie? He never left the parish."

31

"He couldn't afford to."

"That can't be the reason. Tell me."

Where to begin? Of course, she hadn't known Martin as a boy, but he had retained the look of the urchins who had been one of her crosses. At first she thought he was reading her mind when he said he would like to serve Mass.

"A priest should be assisted, Mrs. Murkin. The Mass loses something when the priest does everything for himself."

Marie bristled at this implicit criticism of the pastor. She explained to Martin that with the changes in the parish, there just weren't a lot of little boys around anymore. Or girls either, she added, as if to sound him out on the subject of altar girls.

"I used to be an altar boy here."

"With the Franciscans."

"Of course."

"Father Dowling doesn't belong to an order."

"The cardinal does."

They actually had a little argument, Martin presuming to lecture her on the varieties of priest. "A religious takes vows. That makes a difference."

"The Franciscans were still here when I came."

"Mrs. Murkin, please don't think I'm crit-

32

icizing Father Dowling. Do you think I should talk to him?"

"About taking vows?"

Martin simpered. "Would you raise the matter with him?"

"Maybe you'd better do it yourself."

Afterward, she had thought of a preemptive strike, warning the pastor about Martin. It was difficult to know how to put her objections, though, so she had waited in silence, and prayed. And Martin had spoken to Father Dowling. The one great consolation was that the pastor saw the wisdom of consulting her on the matter.

"The camel in the tent," Marie said tersely.

Father Dowling stopped in the process of relighting his pipe and looked at her through clouds of smoke. Marie loved the smell of pipe tobacco, not that she would say so. How could she then complain of the mess it made, tobacco scattered about, ashtrays overflowing — those usually containing Phil Keegan's cigar ends as well.

"He smokes?"

"You know what I mean. Ask Edna." This last was an inspiration. If there was anything Marie and Edna agreed on, it was Martin Sisk. "When he isn't talking about his late wife he is flirting with the widows." It was thus that Edna captured Martin Sisk in a sentence.

Martin spoke to the pastor, and Father Dowling went on saying Mass without a server. When it was clear the danger had passed, Marie asked what had happened.

"I found out he has arthritis."

"*Does* he?" Marie had arthritis herself, but in Martin's case it seemed a punishment.

"He said Dr. Dolan might want to serve Mass, too."

"That would have been different."

"Maybe I should agree."

It was a tempting thought, but not if alpha meant omega, too. The Dolans had been members of the parish and been married in the church, but affluence had taken them to the suburbs along with so many others. That and the Franciscans, or so Marie liked to think. Of course, the Dolans' connection with St. Hilary's antedated her own time as rectory housekeeper. Now, retirement and nostalgia had drawn them to the senior center.

"Let sleeping dogs lie," Marie advised.

"And camels?"

5

Marie looked around the door of the study and announced that Dr. Dolan wanted to see him, unable to conceal her delight.

"So you make house calls?" Father Dowling said when Marie ushered the doctor in.

"Not likely. I was an anesthesiologist."

Baldness had become a kind of fashion, but not every boy who shaved his head had the noble shape of Henry Dolan's, high domed, seemingly tanned. Father Dowling was tall, but Dolan was taller.

"You still smoke?" Dolan said.

"You make it sound temporary. Please sit down." Behind him, Marie pulled the door closed.

"Everyone smoked when I was young."

"Nine out of ten doctors."

"You remember that."

This initial exchange had not been a guarded sermon. Dolan brought a large hand downward over his face, stopped it, and looked at Father Dowling over his fingers.

"My family has a problem, Father."

The best response to that was receptive silence.

Dolan took a breath. "I had best start at the beginning."

He did, and went on to the end. At first his words had a rehearsed air, but soon he was speaking from the heart. His granddaughter was adopted, something that had never seemed to bother her before, but now she wanted to know who her real parents were. He repeated the phrase.

"You can imagine what that phrase does to my daughter and son-in-law."

"What explains the sudden interest?"

"She has become serious about a young man."

"Ah."

"I have to tell you that I understand why she would want to know. Of course I sympathize with my daughter, but it isn't a criticism of her and her husband. I'm sure it isn't intended to be. Martha is a wonderful young woman. I couldn't possibly love her more than I do."

"I suppose it would be easy for her to find out nowadays."

"Not in her case. There wasn't any agency involved. It was all quite legal, of course." He paused. "Do you know Amos Cadbury?"

"Amos and I have become friends."

"He took care of everything."

"Then I know it was all legal."

"Legal but informal."

Other people's problems are sometimes difficult to see as problems. Why should the Lynches feel devastated because their adopted daughter, now a young woman, wanted to know her true origins? If she was about to marry, their relationship would change in any case. No doubt the young woman's curiosity seemed an implied criticism, as if she regarded the Lynches as impostors.

"My wife is almost as upset as my daughter."

It seemed plausible that women would feel more strongly than men about such a thing. Father Dowling said this aloud.

"Not than George Lynch."

"The foster father?"

Dolan winced. "I have never heard him called that before."

"St. Joseph was a foster father."

"I don't think George would take comfort from that."

"So what do you think will happen?"

"I haven't the faintest idea." He smiled, an unhappy smile. "That is why I hesitated about coming to you. Whatever happens will happen, I suppose. Difficult as it might

37

be in her case, I am sure that, with the proper help, Martha could find out what she wants to know."

"Is your daughter your only child?"

"Oh no. There is Maurice." He seemed to consider saying more but added only, "He is another story."

Portrait of a man whose hopes for his children had been but imperfectly realized. Father Dowling caught the implications of that "another story."

"I could talk to Amos Cadbury."

"Would you do that? I thought of going to him myself but dreaded the role of the interfering grandfather. It would be different in your case."

"I will see Amos. And then we can talk again."

Dolan actually seemed relieved when he stood. He paused. "Sometimes I think of taking up smoking again myself. It can scarcely affect my longevity."

"I won't tell the surgeon general."

Two days later, Father Dowling had dinner with his old friend Amos Cadbury, often referred to as the dean of the Fox River bar. Father Dowling mentioned the Dolans and then asked about their son.

Amos sighed. "Ah, Maurice."

The account Amos gave suggested that he had given thought to the difficulties of his friend Dr. Henry Dolan. "Father, the dark side of doing well when one has risen from the most modest of beginnings is that one's children are apt to be spoiled by the lack of a sense of insecurity."

The Dolans had been blessed in Sheila, Amos added, and George was in every way the son-in-law Henry would have chosen. A medical man, soon at the top of his specialty, a solid and faithful husband. But no life is without its trials, and for the Lynches it was Sheila's inability to carry a child to term. That great gap in their lives had been closed by the adoption of little Martha, and both Henry and George had been present at the birth, Henry administering the anesthesia, George just standing by. Henry had told Amos in a husky voice that he would never forget the image of George taking the newborn child in his arms. What a contrast between his son-in-law and his son.

Maurice had managed to get into DePaul after Henry had a talk with the university's director of development. "Of course, I wrote a letter of recommendation," Amos said. "Ah, the letters of recommendation I have written for that boy."

"Boy."

"Of course you're right. He will soon be forty."

Henry Dolan's name was soon added to those supporting the university fund drive. Maurice hadn't lasted a full year. Perhaps it was just as well. Not even a father's blindness could enable Henry to imagine Maurice as a doctor.

"The fact is they had spoiled him. What want or whim of Maurice's had ever been denied? I suppose that at first it seemed innocent indulgence, and always there had been the hidden hand of the father making things easy for the son." Amos had seen on the wall of Maurice's room a photograph of him in Wrigley Field, in the center of the picture, surrounded by the Cubs, ten years old and wearing a uniform. Half the players had signed the picture. There were signed baseballs as well, even one from the White Sox. Maurice had loved uniforms, even the military uniform of the school in Wisconsin from which he was expelled for misdemeanors neither Vivian nor Henry wanted to hear about. They agreed that the discipline at the school was foolishly demanding, certainly not Maurice's cup of tea.

"My sympathy for the Dolans never wavered, Father, and I will tell you why. I feared that I might have acted as they did if we had ever had children."

"I doubt that, Amos."

"I will never know."

When his school days had ended after two quarters of grades featuring letters seldom seen on a transcript, Maurice was set up in an apartment on the Near North Side, the better to look for suitable employment. He interviewed well. He made a marvelous first impression. All he lacked was ambition and a desire to work. The list of companies by which he had been briefly employed made a sad litany. The truth was that Maurice had no worry about his future. Henry's success ensured that.

Maurice laughed when Henry threatened to cut him off. "It can't be done. I'm your heir."

"I'll give everything I have to charity."

"No you won't."

He was right. It was too late to reverse a lifetime of indulgence.

One day, Vivian stopped by Maurice's apartment. The door was opened by a woman.

"A floozy," she reported to Henry, shuddering. "Brazen. And the way she asked me who *I* was."

Henry cut off Maurice's rent money and

stopped his allowance, bringing an apparently contrite Maurice home.

"She's nobody," he said when Henry demanded to know who the girl was.

"Is she living with you?"

"Of course not."

But Maurice was a stranger to the truth. "For God's sake, son, consider your soul. You're on the path to perdition."

Maurice hung his head. Did the boy still believe anything? "I've been thinking of becoming a nurse."

Henry just stared at him. This was not a young man he would want near any patient of his. Why couldn't he be like his sister, Sheila?

"I guess that isn't realistic."

Amos paused. "Father, the one thing Maurice did well, very well, was golf. He won club tournaments. He almost qualified for the Open as an amateur." Good as he was, though, his performance was far below that of the pros.

It was golf that took him to California. After several weeks, he telephoned, excited. "I have found my niche, Dad."

His niche was a driving range in Huntington Beach. The owner needed a partner. The place ran itself. It was a gold mine. Henry came to Amos to discuss the proposition.

"Why does the owner need a partner?"

"Expansion. There's an opportunity to double the business."

Amos had flown to California. The location of the driving range seemed excellent. The adjacent land could be acquired. Sprucing up the place would help. Amos was able to report to Henry that he had never seen his son so serious. But the proposed partner, Hadley Markus, was not a man to inspire confidence. He had the moist eye of a drinker. His stomach looked like a bass drum hanging over his belt. He needed a shave.

"Could you buy him out?" Amos asked Maurice while they dined at a hotel.

"Are you serious?"

"Find out."

Markus was interested in the proposition. In the end, he stayed on for a time as manager, wanting to continue to occupy the little office where he had spent so many years. Amos flew home, looking out over the cloud cover, praying for the Dolans' sake that Maurice had grown up at last.

With Henry, Amos went over the papers he had brought from California.

"We'll want to make sure there is no lien on the property. I am having that checked. Otherwise, it seems sound." Then he looked

43

steadily at Henry. "The fly in the ointment, I need not say, is Maurice."

"I know. But he seems truly determined to make a go of this."

There was to be a silent partner, Catherine Adams, another transplanted Chicagoan.

"Just a friend?" Amos asked.

"With Maurice, it seldom goes beyond that."

So the deal went through. Maurice took up residence in California. Just having him out of the city was a relief, but the apparent success of the driving range was the first good news Maurice had given them. Now their attention could be concentrated on Sheila and her little family. Then, within a year, the problem with Martha had arisen.

Amos's oral dossier on Maurice Dolan being ended, Father Dowling asked the lawyer if he remembered when the Lynches adopted a daughter.

"Of course I remember, Father. I took care of it for them, the legal side."

"So it must be a matter of record."

Amos tapped the end of his nose with an index finger. "I made an effort to keep the Lynches out of the record. The main concern was the mother's consent. Unless someone knew who the mother was, they would find it very difficult to learn who had adopted the baby. Don't get me wrong. Everything was absolutely *comme il faut.*"

"So Martha Lynch's curiosity will be thwarted."

Amos was silent for a long minute. "Things are more complicated, Father. A week ago the birth mother, in the phrase, came to see me."

6

In her senior year, Madeline took a course in philosophy, imagining that it would address large questions, but it turned out to be a semester devoted to the problem of universals. Is there some man apart from individual men? If not, how does the term keep the same meaning when all the individuals have been replaced by others? At first Madeline was disappointed, but then it became a strange kind of fun, like working crossword puzzles. Besides, her instructor, Mark Lorenzo, was fascinating, shortish, bearded, forever raking his right hand through his beard while he made wild gestures with the other, as if trying to pluck a universal from the air. Students called him Professor As It Were, his favorite phrase, as if he were determined to avoid black and white. He was the youngest instructor in the department. And he was impressed by her midterm.

"What is your major?"

"Computing science."

"Ye gods."

"You don't approve?"

"Have you ever heard of Ramon Lull?"

"No."

"Of course not."

"Who was Ramon Lull?"

"One of the first to go nuts about computing."

"How did you become a philosopher?"

"I didn't. I teach philosophy. As it were. There's a difference."

"Is there?"

"Of course, I could take the Pythagorean dodge."

"It sounds like a dance."

He ignored her. "The philosopher isn't wise, just someone who loves wisdom. The unattainable ideal."

He was even more interesting in his office than in class, and she got into the habit of dropping by. There were no photographs of a wife or children. Just an observation; the events of the year before had turned Madeline into a vestal virgin. She would never marry.

The first time she visited the Women's Care Center, Mrs. Lonum had told her that women who had abortions often observed the date of the deed as if it were a birthday. "It helps to think of the child in heaven." Madeline had no doubt she was pregnant, but it was very early and it still seemed an abstract problem. She had talked to a counselor on campus, putting her problem as a roommate's, and been urged to persuade her to take care of the problem as soon as possible. It seemed odd to hear pregnancy discussed as a disease.

Well, she had her baby and she would always remember its birthday, even though she did not even know if it was a boy or a girl. Whichever it was, her baby was in good hands with the lovely woman she had met before giving birth. When Madeline returned to campus she tried to imagine that it hadn't happened, but she would never be able to do that. She didn't want to.

Catherine Adams, her roommate, opened the door and looked her over from head to foot. Then she opened her arms and Madeline stepped into them. A silent embrace, that was all, and it was everything. It was Catherine who had helped her keep it all a secret from her parents, Catherine who had thought she was crazy to have the baby. She didn't have to say it; Madeline knew. But she knew as well that Catherine would accept her decision, just as she accepted her back without comment and with that one wonderful embrace that said all that needed to be said.

"Be careful," Catherine had said when Nathaniel first became a presence.

"I'll do even better. I'll be good." How ironic to remember that now.

"But will he?"

It wasn't jealousy, as it would have been with just about every other girl. Catherine really didn't like Nate.

"What is it, his sloping forehead, his close-set eyes?"

Nate's forehead was noble, and his gray eyes seemed to mirror her soul.

"No, something about the mouth." And Catherine had laughed, and that was that.

Madeline did not comment on Catherine's taste in men. The first time Maurice Dolan came calling for Catherine, Madeline had understood the attraction. Maurice was tan and athletic; he had met Catherine on the golf course.

"What does he do?"

"Oh, the life he has led." Catherine laughed.

"How old is he?"

"I'll cut off his arm and count the rings."

"He doesn't seem a sturdy oak, Catherine."

Madeline had become all too conscious of the unreliability of charming men. When it happened, when she found she was pregnant, after the initial shock, after the greater shock of Nate's reaction, she found she could tell Catherine of her condition in a matter-of-fact way that made her wonder if she had ever really known herself before.

"And?"

"I'm going to have my baby."

"Oh, Madeline, think."

"I've done little else for days."

"But how?"

"I've been to a place that will take me in. The Women's Care Center."

"I keep forgetting you're Catholic. So is Maurice. In a way."

Catherine was angular of body, but like a model, and her hair was long and straight, always damp in the morning from her shower, drying into the auburn sheen that explained why she wore it so long.

"I forgot, too."

"Oh, how I hate that man."

Madeline thought about it. "Don't, he's not worth it."

"You're right."

When Madeline came back, no worse for wear, her soul marked for life, Catherine made her reentry into student life almost too easy.

"Didn't anyone wonder where I was?"

"You were on leave of absence. You took two courses anyway."

Madeline found that she had gotten a B in programming and an A- in Latin.

"Latin?"

"I figured we could talk religion when you came back."

"I did take Latin in high school."

"Maybe that's why you did so well."

"Catherine, you're marvelous."

"I know."

The funny thing was that Catherine, who had proven immune to Nathaniel's charms, was almost jealous about Mark Lorenzo.

"Don't worry, Catherine, if that's what you're thinking."

"What am I thinking?"

"All right, you're not."

"I took epistemology from him. He seemed to doubt the walls of the room were there until he proved it."

"Philosophy is a game."

"Not for him."

"You're right. Catherine, what would you say if . . ."

Catherine was silent for a moment. "I'd say, 'Go, girl.' I know I would."

"Say it?"

"No. Go."

"You mean it?"

"I'm jealous. Okay?"

"Catherine, everything you do is okay."

Maurice seemed to have disappeared, but Catherine still had a weakness for older men. It seemed that Madeline now did, too.

When they didn't drink the coffee he always had simmering in his office, Madeline and Dr. Lorenzo would go up the street and drink beer in a student haunt. Afterward, they would visit used-book stores, where he seemed more interested in fiction than philosophy. Two weeks before her graduation, he sat across from her, making wet rings on the table with his glass.

"I'm twenty-seven years old."

"I'm twenty-one."

"Do you have a boyfriend?"

"Just you."

He blinked. How she longed to take his glasses and clean the lenses.

"I never thought I'd want to marry."

"Why not?"

"It doesn't mean what it used to."

"I'm Catholic."

"So were all my ancestors."

It went on like that, weird. Afterward, they seemed to be engaged. Madeline had had all she wanted of romantic men. Mark Lorenzo, whose head was in the clouds, had his feet on the ground.

"You have all the luck," Catherine said. "First bad, now good."

They married in the chapel of the Newman Club. Her parents came from California; the rest of the pews were filled with Lorenzos from New Jersey and colleagues and some students, Catherine among them, the reappeared Maurice Dolan at her side. Two years later, Mark published his first book, a reassessment of Ramon Lull, and Stephen, their first son, was born. Birthdays and publication dates were both commemorated in the Lorenzo home. Mark got tenure. They had four sons, and his fifth book was scheduled for publication. After graduation, she saw Catherine infrequently. Catherine was working as a broker in the Loop.

"And Maurice?"

"He's one of my clients. He has brought me lots of business."

"Lucky you."

Catherine grew serious. "Up to a point."

"Maurice is just a client?"

"Nosey."

Catherine had remained unmarried and took vicarious delight in Madeline's fecundity. "You Catholics are terrible." But she smiled when she said it. Mark was nice to Catherine, but little more. Well, Madeline didn't want him smitten by the successful broker Catherine had become.

So the years passed, and then the Monster reappeared.

That is how she thought of him, when she thought of him at all, the Monster. Nathaniel Fleck, the boy who had made her pregnant and then fled in terror when she told him. It had been their last conversation. He did offer to pay for an abortion. It was painful to think that she had been flattered when he took her out. He was a big man on campus, wrote a column for the daily, was on the tennis team, could have his pick of coeds, and he had chosen her. He had everything but character. He didn't want to grow up. "We're too young," was the way he put it. Listening to his self-centered agonizing and his not very subtle suggestion that it was really her fault, she knew she had never loved him. She had liked him because others did; she had enjoyed the suppressed sighs of other girls when they looked at him. But she was only an episode, and when she told him she was pregnant, the episode was over. That was one of the few good results of her trouble.

"Madeline?"

She was in a bookstore looking for early editions of Henry James for Mark's birthday. Was it only imaginary that she recognized his voice after so many years? The man she faced was the boy that was,

54

changed but not altered, still handsome in a world-weary way. He saw that she knew who he was.

"Can we talk?"

"No."

"Please."

She left the store, felt like running up the street, disappearing. How horrible to run into him like that. What in God's name was he doing in Evanston? It wasn't fair.

He caught up with her. She stopped, turning toward a store window where she could see their reflections, watch herself listen to him, see the body language with which he spoke. There was something like real contrition in his voice. They went to Baskin-Robbins, where she bought a cone, paying for it herself, then sat as if she were a mother confessor and Nate her penitent. Admit it, there was a sense of belated triumph.

"What happened?" he said.

"I married and lived happily ever after."

"You know what I mean."

"Do I?"

"The last time we talked . . ." His smile was wistful. There were streaks of gray in his hair, very distinguished. She said nothing. He leaned toward her. "Did you?"

"Yes."

"Which? I have to know."

"Do you?"

"I don't blame you for hating me."

"Don't flatter yourself. I haven't thought of you for years." It even sounded like a lie. "Look, I am not going to tell you anything. Understand? You made your choice way back then and that's that."

He sat back. "You had the baby, didn't you?"

She scrambled to her feet and rushed out of the store. A bus pulled up, and she got aboard and turned to watch the door shut on him. She never rode the bus and had no idea what the fare was. The driver was a boor, but she could have kissed him. As she looked for a seat she could see the Monster standing on the curb, disappearing into the past from which he had come.

Three days later, she got a letter from him, typed. She opened it, unsuspecting, and when she saw "Nate" scrawled at the bottom of the page, she folded it and put it in the pocket of her housecoat. Mark was at the head of the table, their sons like olive plants on either side.

"Who's it from?" Mark asked.

"An old classmate."

"Catherine Adams?"

"Why on earth did you think of her?" It

had been a long time since they had seen Catherine. Her Christmas cards now came from California.

"It is funny. I don't remember most of the students I had last semester."

"But you remember Catherine."

"She was nuts about me."

"You know, she was. But you liked me."

"It was your mind."

"Uh-huh."

"What there was of it." But he kissed her when he said it.

When the kids had gone off to school and Mark to his office, she read the letter. No salutation.

Forgive me for the other day, but I have to know. For years I have thought about what I did to you, and hated myself, and there isn't anything I can do about that now, but I can take responsibility for our child . . .

She crumpled it, crying out as she did so. She stuffed it back into the pocket of her housecoat. Later, she put it in the book she was reading. Trollope's *Kept in the Dark.* But it was insane to keep it. It was like an evil presence in the house. Two days later, she took it into the kitchen, where she burned it and washed the ashes down the disposal, which roared like a clinic's suction machine.

What in God's name was she going to do? Then she remembered Amos Cadbury.

7

When Madeline Lorenzo was announced, the name meant nothing to Amos Cadbury, but as soon as she came into his office, the years fell away and he recognized her. The expression on her face told him that there was trouble on the horizon.

"Do you remember me?"

"Your name wasn't Lorenzo then."

"Well, it is now. I am a married woman with a husband and children."

"That is a blessing."

It would have been nice to think that she had come simply to tell him that, after that crushing incident years ago, life had been good to her.

"Yes, it is. I never told you who the father was."

"That wasn't necessary."

"He has looked me up. He wants to know about the baby."

"What can you tell him?"

"Nothing. Even if I knew, I would tell him nothing. He abandoned me, he let me bear the burden all by myself, and now he claims to feel remorse and wants to make it up to the child."

"Tell him there is no need of that. The child is now a young woman."

She sat back. "To think I have a daughter."

She shook her head slowly, a wondering look on her face. She had grown more beautiful with age. "I have four sons."

"God is good."

"Yes." Suddenly she was anxious. "What can he do?"

"How did he find you?"

She thought about it. "I don't know."

"That couldn't have been easy."

"Can you stop him? His name is Nathaniel Fleck."

"That sounds familiar."

"Do you read novels?"

"He is an author?"

"Yes."

"Have you read him?"

Obviously, she would have liked to lie, but she nodded. "The first time I saw one of them on display at the library, I couldn't believe it. I found several others listed in the catalog. I would never have brought them into my home. I read them in the library."

"And?"

"It's stupid, but I studied them for clues,

some indication that he remembered so I could hate him more."

"Your husband doesn't know?"

"No! It would kill him. I never even considered telling him."

"There was no need."

"That's what I told myself. Now I almost wish I had. There is no one I can talk to about this."

"You can talk to me."

"Someone should warn her."

"That isn't necessary. At any rate, it is premature."

"Mr. Cadbury, he found me. He won't give up. We talked, he wrote to me."

"Do you have his letter?"

"I burned it."

"Good. I am glad you came to me with this. Let me think about it. Meanwhile, don't do anything." He paused. "It might be better if your husband knew."

A cry escaped her. "No, no, you mustn't do that."

"I was thinking of you."

"I couldn't. If you knew him, you would understand."

"What does he do?"

"He's a professor at Northwestern. Of philosophy."

"Philosophy."

"He wouldn't be philosophical about this. Mr. Cadbury, this could destroy us."

"As I said, let me give it some thought."

"You mustn't call me at home. I will call you."

"Of course."

She began to rise, then sat again. "Do you know her?"

"Your daughter?"

"Oh my God." Tears stood in her eyes and Amos prayed that she would not weep.

"You do, don't you?"

Half a century ago, Amos had taken a course in moral philosophy at Notre Dame in which lying was discussed. Speaking, or not speaking, with the intention to deceive. But did everyone deserve to be told the truth? Take a case. The Nazis arrive at the door and ask if there are any Jews in the house. There is a family of them hidden in the attic. What is one obliged to say? There had been unanimous agreement that answering no to such a question was not a lie, since it would be to collude in a crime. The Gestapo had no right to the truth in those circumstances. None of this was helpful to Amos now. He nodded.

"What is she like?"

"You would be proud of her."

"What is her name?"

He thought before saying, "Martha."

"Martha. Martha." As if she could taste the sound.

"Look, the less you know, the less Nathaniel Fleck can learn from you."

"He will learn nothing from me. He isn't even sure I had the baby."

"Good."

He talked with her for another half hour. At his usual rates, it would have been a very expensive visit, but of course he was fulfilling an old obligation to the Lynches. He had tried not to think the name, feeling an absurd superstition that she could read his mind. When she left, he was sure of one thing. She was far more curious about the fate of her daughter than the baby's father could possibly be.

Two days went by, and she did not call. Then Amos read in the paper of the death of Nathaniel Fleck, popular novelist, run down by a car on Dirksen Boulevard in Fox River.

PART TWO

1

Cy Horvath checked it out after the first report of the officer who had been called to the scene, and it was clear that it was hit-and-run.

"He climbed the curb to get him. That's why he spun into the store window," the officers reported.

"He?"

"The guy who got hit."

"You said he climbed the curb."

"The driver."

"Someone say it was a man?"

Liberati, the officer, thought about it. "No."

"You sure?"

"Nobody said the driver was a man."

Horvath talked to the witnesses Liberati had gathered. Two said it was a man, one a woman. Lots of help. Everyone was sure the vehicle was an SUV. A guy with a single luxuriant eyebrow said it was a big one.

"Not a Hummer," said the store owner. This was Schwartz, who couldn't shake off the horror of what he had seen. "He came sailing toward my window, looking right at me, then boom, he was halfway in the store."

Schwartz ran a little coffee shop that featured oddball blends. Cy ordered a cup.

"What kind?"

"Coffee."

"Gotcha." He yelled something to the girl behind the counter. "All right to clean up?"

"I'll help."

Tables had been overturned; there was glass all over the place. A frightened couple still huddled at a small table in the back. They had seen it happen.

"Heard it, I mean." The boy talked through the bridge of his nose.

"Did you see the driver?"

"Is that what it was."

The girl said, "I heard the motor roar when he took off."

"He?"

"The driver."

So the gender of the driver remained undetermined. Schwartz brought him a paper mug of coffee. "That's Colombian."

"How much?"

"On the house." Schwartz looked around, his mustache going up and down. "The house. Geez."

Cy took his coffee outside, where Liberati had been joined by another officer and was keeping the gawkers away from the body. Then Pippen, the assistant coroner, she of the bouncing ponytail, arrived. Thank God it wasn't Lubins, her alleged boss. Cy took her to the body.

Pippen was a pro, cool as a cucumber, and Cy was never sure he liked that. Women were supposed to be emotional. Like Lubins, who was a man. Of sorts. Cy took out the victim's wallet.

"Nathaniel Fleck."

"You're kidding," Pippen said.

"You know him?"

"The name. He's kind of famous."

"For what?"

"His fiction. He's a novelist. Was."

"No kidding."

" 'The moving finger writes, and having written, moves on.' "

"That's his?"

"Tell me you're kidding."

"Okay, I'm kidding."

"You're not."

"Have it your way. He's a long way from home."

"California?"

"You peeked."

"His books are all set there."

"You've read them."

"Some."

"How many are there?"

"Look it up."

"I will."

Pippen pronounced Fleck dead; the crew she had summoned zipped him into a body bag and took him away. Pippen stood for a moment on the sidewalk, arms akimbo, looking up and down the street.

"Nice street," Cy said. "Once you clear away the bodies."

"It reminds me of Northwestern." She looked at him. "The school."

"I know."

"You got a ride?"

"No thanks."

"I'm asking."

"How did you get here?"

"I was shopping. Lubins got me on my pager."

"Let's go."

Sitting beside him in the car, she seemed enveloped in perfume. Cy had a thing for Pippen, but that was between himself and God.

"You going to do the autopsy?"

"Yup."

"What a job."

"That's what my husband thinks."

"What's he do?"
"Ob-gyn."
"What's that?"
"Cy, I love you."
"Try to fight it."

2

Amos Cadbury asked Father Dowling to dinner at the University Club. Before they went to their table, Amos had a Manhattan in the library. Father Dowling asked for mineral water. No need to explain; he had told Amos everything. His work on the archdiocesan marriage court had undone him, and drink had seemed the solution. It became the problem. Sometimes he thought he had been looking for a way off the path he was on. His clerical future had seemed bright — everyone said so, he thought so himself — only the brightness dimmed. His problem intensified; he had gone to a place in Wisconsin that handled clerical drinkers, and when he emerged he had been given St. Hilary's. Supposedly the bottom rung of the ecclesiastical ladder, it had turned out to be his salvation. His priestly life seemed to begin when he moved to Fox River. It was his background in canon law that had been the initial basis for his friendship with Amos.

"Apart from the pleasure of your company, I had a reason for wanting to see you."

Father Dowling looked receptive.

"After dinner."

Their table gave them a lovely view of the city, even a glimpse of the lake. The service was exquisite, the food wonderful. Amos ordered a bottle of wine. The conversation was light, but Father Dowling sensed that Amos was troubled. When they were finished, they returned to the library, where Amos ordered a brandy.

"Dutch courage," he said.

"Living below sea level requires courage."

"I hope you're in the mood for a long story."

Father Dowling got comfortable. "What is it?"

"I needn't say that this must be confidential."

"Of course."

"As it happens, we've already discussed this. In a way. It concerns a client. A woman." Amos sipped his brandy and closed his eyes for a moment. "It was a case I was happy to take. It meant saving a baby."

"Ah."

"You know the statistics, Father. Literally millions of abortions, a slaughter of the innocents. It's barbaric. This was a chance to save one of them. The young woman had the good sense not to abort her baby, but she decided not to keep it either. Arrangements were made to place the child in a good family. The girl went back to school. It seemed a happy ending."

"Wasn't it?"

"That was years ago. The other day, the woman came to see me. She is married, has a family. I hadn't seen her since I helped with the arrangements for her little girl." Amos paused. "I don't think she even knew the baby was a girl."

"You told her?"

"I told her the child's name is Martha."

"Ah. And now she wants to see her child."

Amos shook his head. "I wish it were that simple. No, it's the father who wanted to see his child after all these years."

"He came to you, too?"

"He wrote me a letter." Amos took an envelope from his jacket pocket and handed it to Father Dowling.

Dear Mr. Cadbury,

Many years ago you arranged for the child of a girl named Madeline to be adopted. I am the father of that child. I treated the mother abominably and for years drove from my mind what I had done. The mother is now well settled in life, and I have no desire, quite the opposite, to cause her any further harm. But I have become obsessed with the need to see my child, boy or girl, I know not. You will know. I do not contemplate a confrontation. I would never tell her who I am, but I must see her. Please tell me that I may come speak with you about this. Any advice you may have would be gratefully received.

"The signature is quite a scrawl."

"It is 'Nathaniel Fleck.' "

"I would have to know that to read it."

"Does that name mean anything to you?"

"Should it?"

"It might for several reasons. I have learned that Fleck was a successful author."

"Was?"

"He was run down by a car here in Fox River two days ago."

"Good Lord."

"He had contacted the mother. She came to me in great distress. You can imagine what she thinks of him — did I say that he abandoned her in her trouble? She was furious that he had looked her up."

"Then she didn't tell him to see you?"

"She would have done nothing to indulge him."

"Then how this?" Father Dowling lifted the letter.

"Obviously, he was a very enterprising man. After all, he found the girl. Finding me would have been more difficult, but not impossible."

Amos sipped his brandy and fell silent. Father Dowling waited for him to speak again.

"You can imagine what I am thinking."

"Say it."

"The way the woman spoke of him makes it credible that she would have done anything to stop him."

"Run him down?"

"Anything. If he had continued to try to see her . . ."

"Threatening the life she now has."

"Exactly. So, what must I do?"

Giving advice is more difficult than receiving it, and few are able to do even that. Father Dowling was not eager to tell Amos what to do. The fact was it was not clear what that might be. The lawyer's suspicion that a woman had run over the man who had abandoned her years ago and now had returned to menace the family she had formed was only that, a suspicion. In any case, there was no need to act on it at once, if at all. Nothing would be lost by seeing what course events might take. He put this into words for Amos.

The lawyer listened but did not himself say anything for a time. Then he sighed. "Just to have spoken with you about this has been a great relief, Father."

"I can easily imagine that."

"One more reason to be grateful for our friendship."

"It is a two-way street, Amos."

"Thank you."

So the evening ended. Driving home, it occurred to Father Dowling that Amos had not said whether or not he would follow his advice.

3

"Sometimes I think Phil Keegan ought to just move in here," Marie Murkin said.

"I could never condone such immorality, Marie."

Off she went in a huff, leaving Father Dowling remorseful for his teasing. Not that he thought Marie would brood about it. Besides, she liked the frequency of Phil's visits as much as he did. Phil had been a class or two behind him at Quigley and had been a casualty of Latin, a must in the preconciliar Church. So Phil had left and been in the service and then became a policeman, rising to chief of detectives in the Fox River Police Department. If Father Dowling could scarcely confide professional secrets in Phil, Phil took satisfaction from keeping the pastor of St. Hilary's au courant with the real world.

"Captain Keegan," Marie said frostily, when she led their frequent guest to the study.

"What's wrong with her?" Phil asked when she banged the door shut.

"Unrequited love."

"What's that, not quite love?"

"More or less."

"Anyone I know."

"Do you know Martin Sisk?"

"Is he still alive?"

"So he says. How do you know him?"

"He had a pharmacy down by the courthouse. A lovely wife, Deirdre. Gone to God, alas. He always quizzed me about Quigley."

"He wanted to be my altar boy."

"If you ever want a server, call on me."

"I don't. But I would if I did."

"How do you know him?"

"The senior center."

"Better warn the widows."

"Oh?"

"I'm kidding. We did get a few complaints, though. He wanted to play doctor to female customers."

"Nothing ribald, I hope."

"Since I don't know the word, I can't say."

"Would you like a beer?"

"Is the pope Polish?"

Father Dowling pressed the buzzer that would sound in the kitchen. Three minutes later, there was a knock on the door.

"Come in."

"You rang."

"Phil has been considering your suggestion. He would like a beer."

"So what's new?"

Father Dowling repeated Marie's question after she left the room.

"The usual. A hit-and-run."

"I read about that."

"Funny result of the autopsy, though."

"How so?"

"What killed him was a sliver of glass from the window he went through. Pierced his neck. Of course, it was the vehicle that hit him that sent him through the window."

"Has the car been located?"

"I am beginning to doubt it ever will be. What usually happens, there is damage to the vehicle, and someone notices, a neighbor, or the owner takes it to a body shop for repairs. Because it was going through the window that killed the guy, there may not even be a mark on the vehicle. Maybe it wasn't even a hit-and-run. I mean, he might have survived just being hit."

"People don't just fly through store windows, do they?"

"Oh, there was a vehicle, and it jumped the curb. The witnesses are useless except for that. But what if a driver just momentarily lost control and climbed the curb and this fellow jumped out of the way, maybe pushing off from the vehicle, thus gaining momentum, and then into the window."

"That's pretty imaginative."

"No, it isn't. Cy came up with it."

"And that is the extent of crime in our fair city?"

"Apart from theft, rape, arson, and a car found in the river where it had been for months with a missing person in the backseat." Phil emptied his glass. "And how is the clerical life?"

"Serene. The altar boy crisis seems to have passed."

Phil had to think before he remembered. He chuckled. "Sisk."

"So now he's back to terrorizing the widows at the center."

4

On his baptismal certificate his name had been recorded as simply Martin Sisk, but at the courthouse his full name was on record, Martin Luther Sisk — something he had managed to conceal from others, though the fact upset him when he thought of it, which was whenever he filled out a form with his name. He had never acknowledged the Luther, the whim of his father who had fallen out with the priests. Arguments had gone on over his head when Martin was young.

"Luther was a priest," his mother would say.

"He got married."

"St. Peter was married."

"What's your point?"

"It was a sly trick to pull on the boy."

His father had named him at the hospital while his mother was still recovering. In those days, women spent a week and more in the hospital after giving birth, and Martin's father had been free to play his little joke. He didn't go to the baptism — he was still punishing the priests with his absence

— so Martin always had his baptismal certificate to back up the simpler form of his name. He had even kept it a secret from Deirdre.

"What a lovely name," he had said to her, breaking the ice. He was just starting out as a pharmacist, and she had come in to fill a prescription that indicated she was having menstrual problems.

"Irish." Her red hair was carroty and frizzled, not a straight strand in the vast halo. A little green ribbon because it was March 17. Her pale skin went with the red hair, but it was her enormous eyes that fascinated Martin. She looked at the plastic tag pinned to his pharmacist's coat.

"Martin."

"After Martin de Porres."

"The black?"

"Was he?"

"Didn't you know?"

"Maybe it was St. Martin of Tours."

"The travel agent?"

He made her a cherry Coke at the fountain, and they sat on uncomfortable chairs at one of the little round tables with a glass top. She was a graduate of Barat College and was working up the street in a store that featured religious books, rosaries, and devotional trinkets of all kinds. On their first date they went to a movie, *From Here to Eternity*, thinking that with a title like that it must have some uplifting message. Deirdre was embarrassed when they came out into the evening air. There had been a lot of adultery in the film.

Martin said, "It was moving when he played 'Taps.' "

"But it was so violent."

He took her arm as they crossed the street. Did she move more closely against him? For a moment, he felt like Burt Lancaster to her Deborah Kerr. The pharmacy stayed open until midnight, so he took her there and they sat at their table. She told him she had spent several months in the novitiate, thinking she was called to be a nun.

"I wanted to go to Quigley."

"What's that?"

"The first step on the road to the priesthood."

"Why didn't you?"

He couldn't just say girls, so he said, "Because I met you."

"Sometimes I feel guilty for not staying."

In later years, Deirdre considered it providential that she had been spared from what convent life became in the wake of Vatican II. She had a somewhat unsavory habit of collecting gossip about errant nuns.

"Luther married a nun," she said, and Martin jumped. "I mean, when they leave, priests, nuns, they imagine marriage is some kind of orgy, so married they have to be."

Their marriage hadn't been an orgy. Deirdre could be classified as frigid according to the books Martin perused between filling prescriptions. He told himself it was a professional obligation to keep up on sexology. Such reading filled his mind with speculation about his women customers. He had opened his own pharmacy, near the courthouse, as if he wanted to keep an eye on the records there. His starched cream-colored coat gave him a medical air, and when he dared he carried a stethoscope in a side pocket. He developed a bedside manner standing behind the counter. A susceptible female could bring him out of his lair in the back of the store. Some women confided in him as if he were a physician, whispering their complaints. Using the stethoscope on their backs was safe, but when he had placed it on the ample bosom of a woman a head taller than himself and turned away like a confessor, his hand had moved and the woman cried out and stepped away.

"I'm sorry," Martin said.

"What do you think you're doing?"

He hurried back behind his counter and felt panic until the woman left the store. It turned out her husband was a police officer, a stubby little man who came in and asked Martin what the hell he meant, feeling up his wife.

"It's a professional matter."

"What the hell is that supposed to mean?"

Martin stood there, speechless, wishing he had gone to Quigley and removed himself from temptation. The cop shook his head in disgust and left.

"What was that all about?" Louise, his stick-figure assistant with the eager eyes, whispered the question, standing very close. He could have worked his evil will on her in the stockroom any time, so of course she held no attraction for him.

"A male complaint."

Deirdre was swept away by cancer at sixty-three, and Martin alternated between dramatic expressions of grief and speculation as to whether he would marry again. The world seemed full of widows, but few of them were concupiscible. Even so, it was pleasant to play the Lothario of the senior center at St. Hilary's. How he envied Henry his Vivian.

"The loneliness is terrible," he told her.

"I can imagine."

"I wonder if you can."

"Have you thought of marrying again?"

"All the attractive women have husbands."

"There is Grace."

Indeed there was. A little hefty, perhaps, but her plush body held promise of carnal delight. Grace had silver hair and moist dark eyes and always spoke as if he were meant to read her lips. The problem was that Martin was sure that one unequivocal move on his part would indeed take him to the altar again. Not a bad thought, when he entertained it at night in his lonely bed, but in daylight he saw the comic side of a man his age as bridegroom. Besides, Grace was in her fifties and might expect things he could not deliver.

"Sanctifying grace," Martin murmured.

"Don't blaspheme," Vivian said.

Well, he had touched some chord in Vivian's heart. It was Vivian who told him of her granddaughter, Martha.

"Deirdre and I thought of adopting."

"I've come to think it is a great risk."

She was encouraged by his sympathy, and he got the whole story.

"Wouldn't it be better if she learned who her mother had been?"

Vivian stepped back. He seemed to have

said the right thing. "You're right, Martin. For all we know, she isn't even alive."

"I could find out for you."

"How?"

He held up his hand and looked wise. "What was her name?"

"Madeline."

"Madeline what?"

"I don't remember. If I ever knew."

"That makes it hard. But not impossible. I'll get on it."

"It has to be done very quietly."

"Trust me."

"And Martin? Don't say anything to Henry."

He locked his lips and threw away the key.

5

Tuttle the lawyer sat in a booth in the Great
Wall of China, Peanuts Pianone across from
him, the table heaped with the remains of
their meal. Peanuts sipped beer. Tuttle, who
drank only hot tea when he ate Chinese, had
the pot to himself. The two friends were silent, as they often were together. Peanuts
was almost autistic, a Fox River policeman
thanks to the pull of his shady family. His
eventual retirement would bring no discern-
ible lessening of activity. Though not so
baldly stated, his assignment was to stay out
of the way of serious police work. But he was
Tuttle's eyes and ears in the department and
thus key to the possibility of employment of
those legal skills not universally appreciated. Peanuts was of little help on the recent
hit-and-run, though.

"More run than hit," Peanuts had reported, and smiled at his own lapidary
phrase. He repeated it, in the manner of
those who have surprised themselves with
wit.

"What's that mean?"

89

Peanuts shrugged. He had been debriefed and that was that. So Tuttle, full of food and awash in tea, sat pondering what chances for himself there might be in all this. The dead man had been an author, a fact that had galvanized the literati in the greater Chicago area. A grand memorial service was in preparation for their fallen brother. There had been newspaper accounts of the incompetency of the Fox River constabulary. Obviously, some fanatic foe of the First Amendment was loose, and the police were doing nothing. Tuttle had leafed through some of Nathaniel Fleck's volumes at the public library and found them unreadable.

He picked up a newspaper from the bench beside him, folded to the story devoted to the great man. There was a photo of the woman described as his companion, come like Niobe, all tears, to grieve for her lost love. Catherine Adams. Tuttle was no more a judge of female beauty than he was of modern art. The woman's hair seemed to be worn in a crew cut, and she looked undernourished and gaunt, yet her features were praised in the press account. Perhaps, like Fleck's books, she was an acquired taste. Tuttle found her no more attractive than his secretary, Hazel.

He shuddered at the thought of the female who made his office a place to avoid. She had laughed mockingly at his suggestion that some opportunity for him lurked in these events. The memorial would be held that afternoon, in a chapel on the Northwestern campus, the alma mater of the fallen novelist. Tuttle wavered between taking a nap and attending the affair. A nap meant returning to his office and locking his door against Hazel, always a risky venture when the flood of contempt for her employer rose high in her enormous breast. The memorial it must be.

Peanuts needed help getting out of the booth. He had been thinner when he sat. Peanuts grunted negatively at the suggestion that he accompany Tuttle, so the lawyer set off alone, sleepy at the wheel of his Toyota. Burying the dead, he reminded himself, was one of the corporal works of mercy.

He stood at the back of the chapel and tried to follow the tributes spoken from the pulpit by a series of writers whose obscurity spurred them to oratorical excess. The star of the proceedings was Catherine Adams, who turned out to be tall as well as thin. Her crew cut was covered by a kind of turban, and she wore a flowing dress that almost seemed a vestment. She remembered when she and the deceased were students on this very campus. She recounted with tasteful indirection their liaison, which had spanned the years since their graduation, irregular but continuous. She said this demurely, and there was a murmur of approval for her brave defiance of bourgeois morality. She ended with a poem, and when she had finished the congregation rose as one to applaud her. Tuttle wished he hadn't come.

In his car, he got out his mobile phone and turned it on. Hazel had been trying to reach him. He called his office.

"Where have you been, you idiot? And don't say the Great Wall. I tried there."

"I've been to a funeral."

"Of your career? A client will be here in half an hour. Be here."

She hung up. Tuttle turned off the phone and fought the impulse to throw it out the window. Was it for this that he had struggled through law school, taking most courses at least twice, and failed the bar exams until the third attempt, when he had come with his sleeves full of notes? But "client" is a magic word. He started the engine and headed to his office.

6

Even as he talked with Vivian, Martin had thought of Tuttle, to whom he had sold antacids for years when he kept his pharmacy. A wiser choice would have been someone like Amos Cadbury, but Martin had no wish to incur great expense. His hope was that he could get Tuttle to look into the matter of the mother of Vivian's grandchild pro bono. Unlikely, but Tuttle's fees could not be high. This thought was strengthened when he found the elevator in Tuttle's building out of service. He climbed the dingy stairs to the third floor and stood before a door bearing the legend TUTTLE & TUTTLE. He entered and found himself confronting a woman who made him wish he'd brought his stethoscope.

"Martin Sisk. I called."

Her smile was carnivorous. "Mr. Tuttle will be free shortly."

The door to the inner office was closed. Martin took the chair the Amazon pointed him to.

"You ran the pharmacy near the court-house," she said.

"Yes, I did." He spoke warily, but he could not have forgotten such a woman.

She coughed. She smiled and coughed again. "I really ought to see a doctor about that."

Martin assumed a professional air. "How long have you had it?"

"Would you take a look?"

He was standing beside her chair, looking into the great cavern of her mouth, when the door opened and Tuttle came in. The little lawyer seemed unsurprised by the scene he had come upon. Martin danced away from the woman.

"Still at it, Martin?"

Tuttle opened the inner door, flicked on the light, and went inside. Martin hurried after him. Tuttle sailed his tweed hat at a coat rack in the corner and it spun briefly on the top, then fell to the floor. Tuttle ignored it, sinking into an unoiled chair behind the cluttered desk.

"Close that door, will you?"

Martin pulled the door shut and sat. This visit seemed a vast mistake. He had planned to condescend to Tuttle, but the little lawyer had him at a disadvantage, bursting in on him while he examined his secretary's throat.

94

"So what can I do you for?"

"Tuttle, I don't think even you can be of help on this."

"Try me."

Where to start? "Does the name Dr. Henry Dolan mean anything to you?"

"Go on."

Martin plunged in, finding his own account garbled. Tuttle listened in silence, encouraging him from time to time with a judicial nod. When Martin mentioned that the matter had been handled by Amos Cadbury, Tuttle sat forward.

"Why didn't you go to him?"

"I decided to come to you."

"Wise move. Cadbury would interpret your interest as a criticism. What is your interest, by the way?"

"Vivian Dolan came to me with the problem. She is greatly vexed by it. The whole family is." He gave Tuttle as much of the story as he knew.

"So what is the point of finding the real mother?"

"To warn her off seeing the daughter she let out for adoption years ago."

"Delicate," Tuttle said. "Delicate."

"Yes."

"There has been no contact with the mother over the years?"

"Apparently none."

"Nor any notion where she may be living?"

Martin shook his head, feeling he was contributing to the description of an insoluble problem. "Could you find her?"

"Of course. Not that it would be easy. But adoptions are legal transactions. They are recorded. Once the mother is identified, we can track her down."

Relief came to Martin Sisk. When he had suggested to Vivian that he would find the birth mother of her granddaughter, he had been prompted more by a desire to have that lovely woman in his debt than by the prospect of success. Failure would have the opposite effect. But now Tuttle spoke of the matter as a mere bagatelle, routine.

"So you want to employ me?"

"I hope it won't be expensive." If it were, he could always dun the Dolans.

"Let's hope not. Meanwhile, I will need a retainer."

Martin took his checkbook from his inner pocket. Tuttle followed this action with interested eyes, then seemed to have second thoughts.

"No need for that at the moment. A token amount will make you my client. Do you have twenty dollars?"

Martin took out his wallet and passed a bill to Tuttle who, disconcertingly, held it up to the light. He pushed back his chair, retrieved his tweed hat, dropped the twenty into it, and clamped the hat on his head.

"How is Mrs. Sisk?"

Martin fell back in his chair. "Haven't you heard? She passed away."

"Jesus, Mary, and Joseph," Tuttle said, baring his head as he did so. "You have my sympathy."

"It's been some years."

"Time is a great healer. You didn't marry again?"

"Oh, no."

Tuttle was on his feet. "Come, Hazel will want you to fill out a form. Just routine."

He held the door open, and Martin went into the outer office. Hazel coughed and turned to face them.

"I will leave Martin with you, Hazel. I am going to start looking into something for him." At the outer door, he paused. "Martin is a widower."

Then he was gone.

7

Madeline read with stunned amazement the newspaper story about Catherine Adams's long-term relationship with Nathaniel Fleck, the slain author whose death had stirred up such posthumous pride on campus. Mark had passed the paper to her without comment. Now he said, "And just the other day . . ."

"Yes."

"Have I become clairvoyant?"

But Madeline was thinking of the way Catherine had put Nathaniel down, warning her away from him. Had all that been a ruse? And, despite her liaison with Maurice Dolan, she had claimed to be smitten by Mark Lorenzo. No; Catherine had been her mainstay during the worst time of her life, someone on whom she could lean. All this business with Nathaniel must have come later. After all, a great deal of time had intervened. Madeline resolved to go to the memorial. No need to mention it to Mark, he would be in class in any case.

Catherine's performance at the memorial stole the show. How little she had changed physically, except for the hair, of course. But her head was covered at the memorial, conferring on her an air of noble suffering. Afterward, Madeline lingered, wondering if she should speak to Catherine.

"Madeline?"

She turned but did not immediately recognize the woman who had spoken her name.

"Janet. Janet Owens that was."

Suddenly the unfamiliar figure was transformed. "Janet!"

"What are you doing here?"

"After the story in the newspaper, how can you ask?"

"Shall we say hello to her?"

"Do you want to?"

Janet studied her for a moment, then shook her head. "Where can we have coffee?"

They went up the street to a student haunt and felt middle-aged as they took their coffee to a far table. For fifteen minutes, they brought one another up to date.

Janet lived in Barrington, was married to an accountant, and had three children, two boys and a girl. "And you married a professor, didn't you?"

"Mark Lorenzo. Why haven't you ever looked me up?"

"I couldn't remember his name." Janet smiled wonderingly. "To think you never left this place."

They got around to Catherine. Madeline said that for her the greatest surprise was this professed devotion to Nathaniel Fleck. "She always hated him."

Janet dipped her chin and looked at Madeline. "You're kidding, right?"

"Kidding?"

"Madeline, when you went home for a semester, she and Nathaniel became a big thing. I mean big. Everyone talked about it. I assumed she had stolen him away from you."

"Oh, we were all through by then."

"Even so."

"She told me she was nuts about Mark."

"Then it's a good thing you married him."

"Tell me more about your kids," Madeline said, desperate to change the subject. Catherine had been a familiar stranger recounting her lifelong passion for the dead author, but Janet's remarks made Madeline wonder if she had ever really known Catherine. Catherine alone had known the reason for her supposed leave of absence from the university, and she felt odd talking with Janet, who, close as she had been, never knew.

"Madeline, we have to stay in touch."

"Oh yes."

"I'm sorry now we didn't talk to Catherine."

"The chief mourner."

Janet made a face. "As a housewife I was shocked. Shocked. Well, I guess it's the way of the world now."

How innocent and normal Janet seemed. There was no dark secret in her past that threatened the peace of her marriage. What would she say if Madeline told her the truth about her own past, told her that Nathaniel had hunted her down and insisted he wanted to find their child? His strange death would take on an ominous significance in the light of all that. Not that she was tempted to unburden herself to Janet. Or anyone else.

Then the unsettling thought came that Catherine Adams knew her secret, that in a way she was as much a menace as Nathaniel himself. What if Catherine decided to look her up? She would remember Mark Lorenzo's name. She knew him; she had been at the wedding. The terrible news of Nathaniel's death had not seemed terrible at first. Reading of the strange incident in Fox River, Madeline's first reaction was relief. Thank God, the Monster was dead. It was not a thought she could hold on to, however, rejoicing in another's death, even someone who had treated her as he had.

The women parted outside the coffee shop, repeating their intention to keep in touch.

Mark was already home when Madeline returned. "Did you talk to her?" he asked.

"I ran into Janet, an old classmate. We had coffee. She lives in Barrington!"

"I meant Catherine. I saw you at the memorial."

"But you had class."

"I canceled it. In honor of our famous alumnus. What did you think of Catherine?"

"It was quite a performance. Janet and I decided not to talk to her."

"You told me once she was your closest friend."

"She was."

"Beware of close friends."

"What do you mean?"

"Just before we married, she came to my office. There was something she felt I ought to know."

Madeline felt that the blood was draining from her body. She stared at Mark.

"She seemed to think it would change things. That I wouldn't marry you." He ran a hand through his beard. "I always wish you had told me."

"Oh my God."

He took her in his arms, and at first she tried to break free. Then she submitted to his embrace, weeping helplessly.

"Oh, Mark, what can I say?"

"You don't have to say a thing."

What a wonderful man he was, knowing all along that she had had Nathaniel's baby and saying nothing. There had never ever been anything in his manner that suggested he knew her secret. Dear God, she could have shown him Nathaniel's letter. He would have known what to do. She thought of the days when she had kept the letter, before she had burned it, days during which he might have come upon it.

"Mark, I went to Amos Cadbury, the lawyer who arranged everything. The adoption."

"Tell me about it later. I've got to get back to campus."

"Why did you come home?"

"To make sure you were all right."

Half an hour later, Madeline opened the door to a handsome man whose blond hair seemed to owe more to art than to nature. His smile was radiant, if questioning.

"Tell me you remember me."

"Maurice! Maurice Dolan."

"Right the first time. I thought of calling first."

"Come in, for heaven's sake."

"That's as good a reason as any."

"How many years has it been?"

"Please." He laughed and studied her. "I won't say you've aged well, but you look wonderful."

"I'll make coffee."

How weird it was that the past seemed suddenly to be rushing into the present. While she made coffee, he looked around the house. He liked the study.

"You married a professor."

"I suppose that's obvious."

"Sometimes I think I was meant for the academic life."

She managed not to smile. What an unlikely professor he would have made. She poured the coffee, and they sat in the living room. He liked the living room, too.

"And you have kids."

"Four sons."

"Hostages to fortune. Isn't that the phrase?"

"And you?"

"Still singular."

She sipped her coffee. "I saw Catherine Adams."

"At the memorial for Fleck?"

"Were you there?"

"Catherine and I came together. Nathaniel was a mutual friend."

"I might have guessed that you live in California." She added, "The tan."

"Tell me everything."

She was trying not to react to the remark about Catherine — the name filled her with murderous thoughts, after what Mark had told her — but Catherine figured prominently in Maurice's account of his life. They were partners of a sort in a driving range.

"So you went to the memorial. Did you know Fleck?" Maurice asked.

"Of course I know his books."

"Of course? I've never read them. I suppose if you know the writer that is an impediment."

"How so?"

"The man gets mixed up in the make-believe."

"You knew him well?"

"We golfed together at least once a week."

"Catherine golfed."

"She still does. As often as not, we were a threesome."

"I'm surprised she never married."

"So is she. But Nathaniel was elusive."

"She paid him quite a tribute at the memorial."

"Ah yes. Well, poetic license. Catherine could write novels herself."

"What do you mean?"

"Sometimes Barkis isn't willing."

"Barkis being Nathaniel."

"I wondered if he had looked you up."

Suddenly the banter they had engaged in seemed menacing. Madeline had succeeded, she thought, in masking her surprise at the things he said, but this question was unnerving.

"Why on earth would he do that?"

"Catherine thought he might."

"Did she suggest it?"

"Hardly. I think she saw you as a rival."

"Now, that is funny."

"I'm glad."

He looked around the room as if he wanted to protect it from something. How much did he know? If Catherine had told her secret to Mark, she might have told anyone. Of course, except for the outcome, it was no secret from Nathaniel, but she could not have regaled Maurice with the tale of her old roommate. Still, it was difficult to think of Maurice as the menace Nathaniel had been.

"When do you return to California?"

He opened his hands. "I have family here, you know. My parents are still alive, thank God. They have put up with a good deal from me. I only wish I could make it up to them."

"How could you do that?"

"By marrying and having a family."

"So this Barkis is willing?"

"Oh, not with Catherine. She wouldn't be their idea of a daughter-in-law." He smiled wickedly. "Nor mine of a wife."

"As I remember, you were once quite sweet on her."

"Oh, that comes easily. Marriage is another thing."

"So your parents will have to wait."

"There is my sister, Sheila, of course."

"She has a family?"

"One. A daughter. All grown up suddenly."

"That happens."

"I always had trouble in that department."

"Is that what brought you back, to see your family?"

"Oh, I just tagged along with Catherine."

"Your business partner."

"My, it is good to see you and to see you so settled and happy."

"Thank you."

He stood. "Well, I'm off to Fox River."

"Fox River?"

"The family."

"And your suddenly grown-up niece?"

"Ah, Martha. She's the only one who never scolds me."

"Martha."

"Martha Lynch."

Somehow Madeline managed the good-bye. She thanked him for thinking of her, for stopping by, said she was sorry he hadn't met her husband and four boys. She watched him lope out to the four-wheeler at the curb. A jaunty wave and then he was gone. Madeline sank into a chair. Martha Lynch!

8

The hit-and-run that seemed not to have been a hit and run intrigued Cy Horvath, and he decided to pursue the matter. All the publicity about the late author made him even more curious. There was no suggestion of an explanation of what he had been doing in the vicinity. He lived in California. What had brought him to Fox River? Now the center of gravity had become the campus of Northwestern, and Cy decided to look in on the memorial.

The grief of others always looks exaggerated, but in this case the excess of praise, most of it given by writers who had not even known the deceased, save through his work, was noteworthy. Catherine Adams was a fascinating figure. Once bereaved widows had flung themselves on the funeral pyres of their lost loves. Now they mounted the podium and talked about themselves. Indeed, much of what the woman said turned on her devotion to Fleck over the years, with the faintest suggestion that he had never really deserved it.

Cy was struck by her recollections of their student days at Northwestern.

When the memorial was over, he left the chapel and walked the campus walks. A lovely campus, so near to Fox River, and yet he had never been there before. Of course, Northwestern athletics were the pits; every now and then a run of success, then obscurity returned. Ara Parseghian had coached here and repeatedly beat Notre Dame, which eventually hired him. The last good coach had gone on to Colorado, where he was now enmeshed in some kind of scandal. The students Cy passed did not look as if they gave a damn about the fortunes of their football scene. He came to a building identified as the alumni center and went in.

A ruddy-faced fellow hurried in after him and announced over the reception counter that the memorial had been huge. "We'll feature it in the alumni magazine." He turned to Cy as if to have his decision endorsed. Then he pushed through a half door and disappeared into an office labeled DIRECTOR.

Cy followed him. The man turned in surprise. Cy showed him his identification. "I am investigating Nathaniel Fleck's death."

The man collapsed into the chair behind the desk on which a name plate announced

MILFORD HAMPTON. A look of meditative wonder came over his face. "An amazing thing. None of the speakers referred to the way he had died. My God."

"What a way to go."

"It was a hit-and-run?"

"That's what we thought at first. Now that's unclear."

"Unclear!"

"Death was not caused by being struck by a vehicle."

"But I read that the maniac climbed the curb and chased him down the sidewalk."

"What I am wondering is what was he doing in the area."

"There I can help you."

"Good."

"He was here, in this office, just days ago. He was anxious to look up old classmates."

"Is that difficult?"

"Not in the case of males. Women marry and change their names. I have Computing working on a correlation system, but it's not an easy matter." He looked beyond Cy. "Women don't bond with an institution the way men do. Often when they marry we don't know, and for years we're mailing things to their parents' home. A total waste."

"Did Fleck have any luck?"

"He did. Another classmate had given him the married name of the person he was curious about."

"A woman."

"What are we talking about?"

"Who is she?"

Suddenly Hampton became wary. "I'm not sure I should give out that information."

"We don't have many leads, Mr. Hampton."

"But what possible relation could this person have to his being killed in Fox River?"

"Probably none. But until I know that I will wonder. It's a nuisance getting a court order . . ."

"Oh, all right." He rummaged around on his desk and came up with a printout. "It's lucky I haven't thrown this out." He scanned the piece of paper. "Here it is. The classmate he was interested in is now Mrs. Lorenzo." He looked up as if Cy had won a bonus. "She is the wife of one of our professors."

"So she lives right here in Evanston."

"That's right."

Cy had his notebook out and waited, pen at the ready. He wrote down "Madeline Lorenzo" and the address. "The husband is Mark Lorenzo. He's in philosophy." He frowned. "I hope you don't mean to give them any trouble."

"No."

"And there should be no need to say how you learned this?"

"Mr. Hampton, he probably looked her up and this will come as no surprise at all."

Hampton seemed relieved. He shook Cy's hand. "You should have seen the memorial for Nathaniel Fleck."

"I did."

9

When Bernard Casey first drove Martha up the long drive to his parents' home in Libertyville, along what seemed a mile of white fencing that separated the drive from vast green acreage on either side, she was astounded.

"It's a farm!"

"Well, a horse farm."

"This is where you grew up?"

"To the degree that I did."

She saw a group of horses far off, large ones and one or two little ones on spindly legs tagging along after their elders. The trees on the far horizon seemed more blue than green, and there was the sweet smell of grass.

"How do you keep it mown?"

"Oh, the horses do that."

If Martha had expected a farmhouse, she had another surprise in store. The term "mansion" is seldom used now, save in historical applications, but the size and grandeur of the Casey home made even the huge and ostentatious houses in the newer suburbs seem modest. The drive brought them under the porte cochere as the doors opened and Bernard's father and mother came out to greet her. Long planned, somewhat dreaded by Martha, this was her presentation to the family.

Of course, she had often seen Bernard's father in the firm's offices, an imposing figure at the end of a corridor, coming in and out, cheerily saying hello but continuing to move toward his inner sanctum, unlikely to be seen again by mere paralegals.

"Vexilla regis prodeunt," Willa had hummed, after Casey senior was out of sight.

"Shame on you, Willa."

"I was thinking of Dante's use of it, not the liturgical."

Willa was a constant surprise. "What does it mean?"

"The standards of the king go forth."

"How do you know these things?"

"My dear, I am a graduate of St. Mary's College, the sister school of Notre Dame. Of course you've heard of Sister Madeleva."

"Did she play football?"

Willa gave her a look. The institutions of higher learning in South Bend, Indiana, shared in the reverence with which Willa held her religious beliefs.

"Is Mr. Casey a Notre Dame alumnus?" Madeline asked her.

"Senior? No. He couldn't afford it." Willa's voice dropped to a whisper. "DePaul."

"Shame."

"It was a better school in those days," Willa said loyally. "Mr. Casey rose from nothing to what he has become."

The posh offices in the Loop had not prepared Martha for the Casey estate in Libertyville. It helped Martha relax to remember Willa's remark about Mr. Casey's humble origins. And Bernard's parents could not have been nicer. First, there had been a tour of the farm in an open Jeep with Bernard at the wheel and his father beside Martha telling her what they were seeing. When they came back to the house, Mrs. Casey took Martha around, speaking deprecatingly of the rooms through which they passed, all looking like pages in a magazine. Martha was struck by the brightness of the interior, the huge windows that framed scenes of the farm. In what Mrs. Casey called the family room, with its big fireplace and timbered ceiling and more huge windows, there were trophies everywhere, little bronze horses mounted on marble, each adorned with a metal plaque recording the

116

achievement it represented. That was where they all sat for coffee.

"Lynch," Mr. Casey said.

"My father is George Lynch."

"The physician?"

"A pathologist. We live in Fox River."

Casey senior nodded. Martha had the impression that he already knew all about her family. He said that he had heard of her father. Martha found herself telling him of her father's decision not to join the staff at the Mayo Clinic, and of her grandfather, also a medical man.

"And what was his name?" Mrs. Casey asked.

"Oh, he's very much alive. Dolan."

"Henry Dolan?" Mr. Casey sat forward.

"Yes."

He turned to his wife. "They're members of the club."

"Vivian Dolan is your grandmother?"

"You know her?"

"Then your mother's maiden name was Dolan."

"Yes. Sheila Dolan."

"My dear, we're practically related."

Bernard spoke as if for the first time. "Ah, I knew it. An impediment. Consanguinity."

"Sheila and I were at Barat together."

"We all went to Barat, my mother, my grandmother," Martha said. "I was the third generation."

Martha supposed that horses were judged like this, by pedigree. The Caseys had welcomed her warmly when she arrived as a stranger, but now the atmosphere was cozy and familial, and their reaction to Bernard's remark indicated that his parents knew which way the wind blew and, having met her, approved.

When they said good-bye, Mrs. Casey held Martha's hand in both of hers and smiled a benediction on her. Mr. Casey cleared his throat and kissed her cheek. Then she was in the car beside Bernard, and they set off down the long driveway.

"Bravo, Martha. You were a triumph."

"I like them."

"More important, they like you."

They went to see the Cubs — a victory, but either way, victory or defeat, would have been fine with the festive fans. Bernard was ebullient and drank too much beer and insisted on thrusting hot dogs and frosty malts and bags of peanuts on her.

"Stop! You'll have to roll me out of here."

Sammy Sosa hit a long home run over the left field fence with everyone in the park on their feet and yelling. As the excitement

118

died down, Bernard turned and kissed her on the mouth.

"You'll owe me one for every home run."

"What about triples?"

"You get to kiss me."

She kissed him then and there, and they sat, their shoulders leaning against one another, alone in the crowd, in love. It was only later, in her apartment, alone at last, that Martha acknowledged that the visit to the Caseys had been a depressing experience.

It was as obvious as could be that their approval of her was derived from her grandparents and parents. Martha they knew not at all, but she came recommended by her antecedents, and that explained the warmth of the welcome and the tenderness of the departure. What would they have said if she had told them the Lynches adopted her, that no Dolan blood ran in her veins? That would have altered the whole visit. She could just keep quiet about it, of course. Some of the sheen of the Dolans and Lynches would still attach to her. After all, they had raised her, and they had sent her to Barat. Short of a blood test, no one would know she was anything other than she seemed to be. No doubt, eventually, it would come out, but that could be years from now, when it wouldn't matter. By then, she would have been accepted for herself, not her supposed relatives. She went to bed resolved to say nothing.

She woke in the morning to find that her resolution had deserted her. She couldn't do that to Bernard. Forget about his family. This was between the two of them. He knew who he was, and her origins were obscure. She simply had to bring it up with her mother again. Now her mother would see how important it was that Martha learn who her real parents were.

10

Before he left the alumni center, Cy Horvath learned the location of Professor Lorenzo's campus office, but when he went out to his car he was undecided whether to call on the professor in his office or on his wife at their home. The two were equidistant from where he was parked, so the matter could not be decided on the basis of convenience. Of course, a good part of his hesitation arose from the thought that he was on a wild goose chase. So he called in, hopeful that a basement full of bodies had been discovered or that some madman at the mall randomly shooting shoppers would provide an excuse to use his time more profitably.

"Nothing much, Cy," Phil Keegan said. "Where are you?"

"Evanston."

"What for?"

"A funeral of sorts."

"Anyone I know?"

"I didn't know the man myself."

"My God, Cy, only the Irish make a point of attending any funeral going."

121

"I didn't see you there."

"I'm going out to St. Hilary's."

"A funeral?"

"To see Father Dowling."

"Give him my blessing."

He got out of the car, locked it, and, since he was facing that way, went to call on Professor Lorenzo in his office.

"Lieutenant Horvath?" The departmental secretary stared at him.

"That's right."

"Is he expecting you?"

"Is he in?"

A bearded face appeared from a doorway down the hall. "Did I hear my name taken in vain?"

"There's a lieutenant to see you."

"Finally! My application for West Point has been approved."

"Are you Professor Lorenzo?"

"Come on in."

Cy felt that he had entered Father Dowling's study, only worse. All four walls were bookshelves, save for a narrow window that was cranked open. On its sill was a stack of books; there were books on the floor, books on the little table next to the easy chair Cy was shown to, books and papers all over the desk. All it lacked was the smell of tobacco.

Lorenzo closed the door. "I only leave it open when girls visit."

Cy nodded. "Nice place."

Lorenzo sat behind his desk, looking around. "It is, isn't it? I have been in this office over twenty years."

"It looks lived in. You teach philosophy?"

"Is this an arrest?" Large teeth emerged from the facial hair when he smiled. "They executed Socrates, of course. Corrupting youth, they called it. My ambitions are not so high. Lieutenant of what?"

Cy handed Lorenzo his identification. He studied it. "Fox River?"

"I came over for the memorial for Nathaniel Fleck."

"I went myself. Once there would have been a religious ceremony of some kind. Now there are only eulogies and empty consolation. 'He will be missed.' " That had been a recurrent phrase in the tributes.

"He wasn't missed on a Fox River street."

"Tell me about that."

"There's not much to tell. I'm investigating it."

"Hence your presence at his memorial."

"I dropped by the alumni center."

"You went there?"

Cy ignored that. "I am trying to figure out

why the man was here. He lived in California. Everyone at the memorial seemed surprised that he had been in the Chicago area."

"And what did you learn?"

"He was trying to locate your wife."

Lorenzo let out a soundless whistle. Then he said, "They were classmates."

"I wondered if he had looked her up."

"Yet you came to me."

"I was on campus. Of course, I'll want to talk to your wife. Did he find her?"

Another soundless whistle. "Why don't we go somewhere for a beer?"

It was called a pub and was a large room with wooden tables and comfortable chairs. Lorenzo brought a pitcher of beer to the table and filled Cy's glass, then his own. The place was half full of students but not too noisy. Lorenzo looked around. "The life of the mind." He lifted his glass. "Cheers."

"Cheers."

But he did not look cheerful when he put down his glass and leaned toward Cy. "I am going to make it unnecessary that you talk to my wife. She and Fleck were lovers while they were students. She became pregnant. He abandoned her. After all these years, he decided to come back and find out if she had had the baby."

"Why?"

"He wanted to be a father. Or to find out if he had been one all along."

"What did she tell him?"

"Nothing."

"And that was that?"

"He wrote her a letter. She burned it."

"Did you talk to him?"

"No."

Cy finished his glass, and Lorenzo refilled it.

"How exactly did he die?" Lorenzo asked.

"It seemed a hit-and-run at first."

"Wasn't it?"

"All that's clear is that a car jumped the curb, hit him glancingly, and sent him through a store window. A piece of glass went through his throat. He bled to death right there."

"So what are you investigating?"

"I wish I knew."

Lorenzo sat back. "There's no need to talk to my wife, then, is there?"

"Does she drive an SUV?"

"What's that?"

"What does she drive?"

"She doesn't. We have a car, but we

seldom use it. I walk to campus. Everything we need is close by."

"But you have a car?"

"Of sorts. At the moment it's in the garage for repairs."

Cy took out his notebook and looked at Lorenzo.

"You want the name of the garage?"

"Yes."

"My God, do you actually think she went after him with a car?"

"I don't think. I'm a cop, not a philosopher."

"Quit bragging. I took the car in a week ago."

Cy thought about it. "I'll check it out anyway."

"After you do, there'll be no reason to bother my wife."

"I'll check it out."

The garage was attached to a filling station. The mechanic's name was Pierce. He looked at Cy's ID, looked at Cy, then said, "Lorenzo. I haven't gotten around to it yet. They said there was no rush."

"Can I see it?"

There were several cars parked along the fence that bordered the station. Pierce took him to a vehicle in need of a wash.

"What kind of car is this?"

"A Neon." Pierce made a face.

"Never heard of it."

"They're made out near Rockford."

"What's it in for?"

"Nothing special. A general tune-up."

Cy looked the car over. It certainly bore no resemblance to an SUV. There were no dents, at least of recent origin. Those there were ancient, covered with dust.

Pierce said, "People just put gas in their cars and expect them to run like watches."

Cy thanked him and left. Driving back to Fox River, he tried to put the whole thing out of his mind. He might have asked Pierce if either of the Lorenzos could have driven the car off his lot while it was waiting for its tune-up, but what was the point? Perhaps he should have talked with Lorenzo's wife, Madeline. As Cy had told the bearded professor, he was not a philosopher, but it is not always easy to keep long thoughts at bay. Imagine having fathered a child and, unable to forget it, even years later, wondering if the child had even been born, if it had been a boy or girl, if it was still alive. Nathaniel Fleck had apparently tried to find the answers to those questions, and now he was dead. These two things seemed connected, but were they? A detective looks for connections between events, but sometimes the only connection is accidental. Had some motorist momentarily lost control of his car, jumped the curb, and somehow caused Fleck to be propelled through that store window to his death? The driver might not even have realized what he had done, to the degree that he had done it, and sped off down the street. All that was possible. But Cy found little comfort in the thought, and he brooded.

11

Sheila listened to Martha's description of her visit to the Casey home in Libertyville, the phone pressed close to her ear, eyes shut, dreading what was coming.

"All they talked about was you and Dad, and Grandma and Grandpa. They were so glad to learn who I was."

"Did you like them?"

"Oh, yes."

"So things are serious between you and Bernard."

"Didn't you like him?"

"We both did."

"Do you remember her? She said she knew you in college."

"I knew her, of course, but we weren't friends."

Silence on the line. Now it would come again, the awful question. It was Martha's love for Bernard that fueled her curiosity, but if it hadn't been Bernard Casey it would have been someone else wanting to marry her and stirring up this desire to know who her real parents were. Real. So small a word could be a dagger in the breast.

"Mom, I felt like an impostor."

"That's nonsense."

"They breed horses. They think in terms of bloodlines."

"You are not a horse, sweetheart."

"Mom, I have to know."

"No, you don't. Martha, it hasn't mattered all these years and it doesn't matter now."

"Did you know her?"

Sheila remembered the lovely girl at the Women's Care Center; she remembered holding her in her arms as they wept. How much like her Martha was. She realized that now as she never had before. When the girl's time came, she was wheeled away, Henry Dolan on one side of her, George on the other, the obstetrician at the foot. An hour later, Martha was put in Sheila's arms, George appeared, and they drove home with their daughter. Oh, the joy they had felt. How cruel it seemed that the memory should now be so threatening.

"Yes, I knew her. Getting to know her was part of it."

"What was she like?"

"You could be her twin."

"Really!" The delight in Martha's voice

turned the knife in Sheila's breast. "Mom, I'm coming home tonight, okay?"

"For dinner?"

"If I may."

"Martha, this is your home."

After she hung up, Sheila tried to cry but couldn't. She seemed far beyond tears. Martha's renewed insistence seemed to launch her into some point in space where nothing was familiar, all was cold and unrelated. *I am her real mother,* Sheila thought fiercely. What is a real mother but the woman who has raised you from an infant, been with you through all the little crises of life, been at your side forever? She almost hated the thought of that lovely girl at the Women's Center, but that would have been like hating Martha.

"We could tell her."

"George!"

"What possible difference can it make now?"

"None. That is the point. Who knows where she is or what she has become? And, George, think of her. Do you suppose she would want this all dredged up now? I would imagine she has spent a lifetime putting this out of her mind. That is what we enabled her to do. Think what it would do to her to have Martha show up on her doorstep, two strangers looking at one another. That would be cruel. We can't do it."

"Martha's not going to forget it."

"There is no way she can find out."

"That sounds cruel, too."

"Only because she has brought it up."

"But she has. You know her, Sheila."

"Could she find out?"

"I'll talk to Amos Cadbury."

"Mr. Cadbury wouldn't tell her. He wouldn't do that to us."

"Sheila, it must be a matter of record."

"Where are the papers?"

It surprised Sheila that George found them so easily. They sat side by side on the couch, looking at the legal record of their adopting Martha.

"South Bend?"

"He seems to have filed the papers there."

"There is no mention of the mother."

"That's odd."

"So we could show her this and she would see there's no way . . ."

After dinner, during which nothing was said of the matter that weighed on all their minds, George, as agreed, brought it up.

"Martha, I have located the adoption papers. We think you should see them."

"Oh yes."

Martha studied the document, turned it

over, read it again. She looked from Sheila to George. "It doesn't say."

"No."

Martha flung the paper from her. "What good is that?"

"Well, it made you ours."

Martha stared at George, and her expression softened. She crossed the room and took him in her arms. "Oh, Daddy."

Sheila could not remember when she had ever seen George cry.

12

The following day, Martha told Bernard about the document she had been shown and the great disappointment it had been. "There was no mention of my mother."

He rubbed his chin. "This is not my sort of thing, sweetie. I have no experience of adoptions at all. But I should think there must be some release on the part of the mother."

"It wasn't there."

"I imagine that was a separate matter, and your parents might not have been given that. No reason why they should have been, I suppose. You say South Bend?"

"Isn't that odd?"

"Wait a minute. I went to school there."

"You know what I mean."

"Who was the lawyer?"

"Amos Cadbury. He's a friend of my grandfather's."

"Cadbury! He went to law school at Notre Dame."

"So you can talk to him?"

"I could, sure, but I'd rather not. Look,

Martha, the paper you saw was registered in Indiana, but any release on the part of the mother must have been made where the birth occurred."

"It must have been Fox River."

"Not necessarily."

"Oh, please don't make it seem an insoluble problem."

"I'll tell you what I can do. If I go to Cadbury, he's going to put some menial on it. I doubt whether he has vivid memories of every legal thing he's done."

"Would there be a record in his office?"

"It could only be a copy. Look, let's bypass Cadbury. At least for now. All we need is some run-of-the-mill lawyer to check it out."

"Do you have anyone in mind?"

"Get the phone book. The yellow pages."

She brought it, and he put it on his lap and began to leaf through. "Ah. Here. A lawyer who puts an ad in the yellow pages is just the sort of man we want." He closed his eyes and dropped his finger on the page. Then he looked. "Tuttle and Tuttle. Never heard of them. They okay with you?"

"Will you talk to them?"

"Will you be my client?"

"For life. But, Bernard, I have to know."

"Then, my darling, you shall."

When she was again free of his embrace, she said, "Oh, I hate being a legal entity."

"We all are."

The only relative she could really talk with about all this was Uncle Maurice, who had suddenly shown up unannounced, spreading apprehension in the Lynches and Dolans. What awful thing was he involved in now? But Maurice had not come bearing bad news. The uneasiness lifted slowly. He took Martha golfing.

"You're not bad," he said afterward, as they lounged in the clubhouse. "With a little work you could be good."

"Oh, it's so good to see you."

"You, too, kiddo. I won't tell you you're beautiful."

"And I won't tell you you're handsome."

"But dissolute."

"Isn't everything going well?"

"The business? Martha, it takes care of itself. You hire a few kids and they do it all. I just hope they're not stealing me blind."

"Now, if you would only marry and carry on the Dolan name."

"I'll leave that to you for the present."

"I couldn't do that in any case."

"I suppose you would have to take your husband's name."

"Maurice, you know it's more than that."

He actually had to think before he understood. Was she the only one who regarded her status as strange?

"Not that old stuff."

"There is someone, Maurice. Someone I love very much. I've met the family. They checked me out as they might have a horse they meant to buy. It was all the Dolans and the Lynches. I made a great hit."

"I can believe it."

"But I'm not a Lynch or a Dolan. I don't know what I am. Even apart from his parents, I could never marry without knowing where I came from."

"Aren't Adam and Eve good enough for you?"

"How would you feel if you found out you had been adopted?"

"Relieved, in a way. I wouldn't be such a disappointment then."

"Please, Maurice. Be serious about this."

He nodded. He lit another cigarette. "So find out."

"Why can't they just tell me?"

"What makes you so sure they know?"

Good Lord, she had never thought of that. She had no clear idea of how adoptions took place. Did people adopt anonymous little babies, unaware of where they had come from, who the mother was? Did that explain the pain her questions caused her mother? Maybe she was in the dark, too, and just didn't like to think of it. But she had told Sheila she could be her mother's twin. Even so, it was so much easier just to think of herself as Sheila's daughter, as a Lynch. Well, what else could she be now? She couldn't live her life over, be raised by someone else.

"You're no help, Maurice."

"It's the story of my life, sweetheart."

"But I love you just the same. You're the best of the lot, you know."

"Good God, what a depressing thought."

13

"Will you take a look at that?" Marie said, standing at the window in Father Dowling's study.

"At what, Marie?"

"At the two of them, hand in hand at their age, and him simpering like a silly boy."

"I don't think I'll get up to see such a scandalous scene."

"Grace Weaver is sixty if she's a day, and as for Martin Sisk . . ." Marie made a disgusted noise and turned from the window with her body but not her head. She continued looking out. "And he wanted to be your altar boy!"

"Altar boys don't take a vow of celibacy, Marie."

"He shouldn't need a vow at his age."

"Come away from the window. Jealousy is an unseemly vice."

"Jealousy!" Marie bounded to the door, where she stood glaring at the pastor.

"It will be our secret."

Marie managed not to slam the door when she left. After a moment, Father

Dowling rose and looked discreetly out his window. There indeed on the walk was Martin Sisk walking hand in hand with Grace Weaver. Such autumnal pairings were not unknown among the widowed denizens of the senior center, a source of mild amusement to Edna Hospers and, in this case at least, of disgust to Marie Murkin. Well, not everyone had Marie's towering self-reliance, but even so she should know what loneliness does to the aged. There was a sharp rap on the door, and he got back to his chair before it opened. Marie looked in, smiling sweetly.

"Guess who's here?" She stepped aside, and Amos Cadbury appeared in the doorway.

Father Dowling rose. "Amos, this is a delightful surprise."

"Forgive me for showing up unannounced. I tried to call you from my car but couldn't get through."

"I never heard the phone," cried Marie. "Did you, Father?" She squeezed past Amos and came to the desk. "No wonder." She jiggled his phone into its receiver. "The line was open."

"Another mystery solved."

"Who knows how many calls couldn't get through?"

140

"Thank you, Marie."

She glanced at Amos, who managed not to intercept her censorious look, and then she was gone.

Amos settled down. "Remarkable woman."

"Indeed."

For Amos, a woman who could cook like Marie was forgiven many things.

"You must join me for lunch. After the noon Mass."

"You will think I have chosen the time out of cunning."

"Marie will be delighted."

"As will I."

He informed Marie that they would be having a guest, eliciting a flood of apologies for the simple meal she had been preparing. If only she had known in advance! She cut short her apologies to scamper back to her kitchen.

"I will wait until later to speak of the reason for my visit," Amos said.

"Of course."

Ten minutes later, Amos went with him to the church, heading for a front pew while Father Dowling readied himself in the sacristy. One of the distractions of saying Mass facing the people is that one more or less unconsciously takes note of who is there. Martin and Grace knelt side by side, across the aisle from Amos. Scattered through the crowd were other regulars at daily Mass, among them the Dolans, far in the back. Afterward, when Father Dowling emerged from the church, he found Amos in conversation with the Dolans. The little group suddenly seemed a middle term, linking what Henry and Amos had told him separately. Father Dowling joined them and considered asking the Dolans to lunch as well, but that would have been straining Marie's hospitality. She could easily stretch what she prepared for him to two, but four would present a problem he might hear about for days.

When they were at table, Marie ladled out potato and leek soup, over which Amos murmured appreciatively, and followed it with an omelet and salad for which he awarded her a *cordon bleu.* They ended with coffee and a slice of Marie's apple pie. The patrician Amos actually kissed the cook when they were done, and Father Dowling thought for a moment she might toss her apron over her face like a character in Dickens. If Martin Sisk was a simpering boy, she was a giggling girl. Then the men settled down in the study, where Father Dowling lit his pipe and Amos broke the routine of his day by lighting a cigar before sunset. There were some minutes of smoke-filled silence.

"You remember our conversation at the University Club, Father?"

"Yes."

It did not surprise Father Dowling that Amos should want to go over what they had spoken of before, nor was he himself reluctant to do so. After all, this was not something either of them could discuss with anyone else. And so he listened to Amos tick off the elements of the story. Martha Lynch's desire to know the truth about her background had upset both her parents and grandparents. But it was the reappearance of the woman who had given birth to Martha that most affected Amos.

"I feel I should have been more forthcoming. I did tell her the child was a girl and that her name is Martha. Why did I stop there?" asked Amos.

"Perhaps if she had pressed you, you wouldn't have."

But it was the dreadful suspicion that had been stirred in Amos's mind when Nathaniel Fleck was killed on Dirksen Boulevard that explained the lawyer's need to have this conversation.

"You haven't told anyone else, have you, Amos?"

A thick blue smoke ring issued from Amos's mouth and drifted across the study. "I took your advice."

"And wish you hadn't?"

"Somewhat."

"Amos, the police aren't sure it was a hit-and-run. The whole incident turns out to be very ambiguous."

"The man is dead."

"That's true enough. But not that someone was clearly responsible for it."

"Father, even if I thought Madeline Lorenzo had killed that man, I don't know that I would go to the police."

There were things he might have said, but it seemed better to subside into silence. Amos blew another smoke ring. Smoke curled upward from the bowl of Father Dowling's pipe. They might have been sending up prayers that all would be well with Martha and the Lynches and Dolans — and Madeline Lorenzo. Father Dowling added a prayer for the repose of the soul of Nathaniel Fleck.

14

Only his irrepressible spirit had prevented Tuttle from succumbing to professional despair. For him to have become a lawyer at all amounted to such a feat that the largely rocky road he had trod since finally passing the bar exams seemed a smooth slide into obscurity. When doubt did strike, he was sustained by the thought of his father — his honorary posthumous partner in TUTTLE & TUTTLE — who had never lost faith in his son's dogged pursuit of a legal career. Now, from the beyond, his paternal parent remained his recourse, one he frequently consulted and on whose intercession he counted to keep his head above water. Success had been rare, but whenever apparent shipwreck threatened, Tuttle senior had come through. Now there seemed a veritable avalanche of good things turning up.

Item. Martin Sisk. Not only had the erstwhile pharmacist become a client, he was diverting the amorous attention of the redoubtable Hazel.

"Look out for his hands," Tuttle had warned.

"Tuttle, you wouldn't know a gentleman if you met one." If Hazel had been capable of blushing, her cheek would have been suffused as she said it.

She and his new client had gotten onto the subject of old films, and it turned out Martin had quite a collection.

"He has a DVD of *From Here to Eternity.*"

He had asked Hazel to his place for popcorn and a movie — prompting Tuttle's warning and her contemptuous response.

"What exactly has he hired you to do?" Hazel asked her boss.

"Just a routine matter."

Hazel gave him a look. "Well, I knew it couldn't be a federal case."

So he told her nothing and began exploring the antecedents of a young woman named Martha Lynch. At first, Tuttle thought Martin was pulling his leg. Everyone knew Dr. George Lynch and wife. But Martin had put his arms on Tuttle's desk and whispered, "Martha Lynch was adopted."

"There's no law against that."

"I want you to find her mother."

"Mrs. Lynch?"

146

"Her birth mother. The woman who bore her."

Tuttle pulled a legal tablet toward him and licked the end of his pencil. "Go on."

The adoption had taken place twenty-two years ago. Martha had been born in Fox River, her mother having resisted the idea of an abortion thanks to the support of the Women's Care Center. Tuttle was to find the woman.

"There has been no contact between her and the Lynches since?"

"Vivian Lynch has no idea what became of the woman."

"And when I find her?"

"You're sure you can?"

Tuttle chuckled.

"Good. Just give me the information. Don't talk to the woman, don't let her know she has been found. Just let me know. The Lynches will do the rest."

"And Amos Cadbury handled the matter?"

"Yes."

Someone with more standing in the profession would simply have gone to Cadbury and talked it over, lawyer to lawyer, but this path was closed to Tuttle. If Cadbury had his way, Tuttle would have been disbarred the first time he had come under review by the local bar association, but Tuttle senior had intervened and that evil day had been avoided, twice. The mention of the Women's Care Center suggested an alternative. Within an hour of talking with Martin, he had pulled into a parking space at the center and bustled inside. His entrance caused a stir. A woman rose from behind the reception desk and hurried to him, a worried look on her face.

"Can I help you?"

"Are you the manager?"

She took his arm and led him out of the reception area with its obviously distraught young women. In the corridor, she stopped. Her name tag read MARJORIE. Tuttle took off his tweed hat and fished out a card and handed it to her. She read it with concern.

"Whatever your business, you should take it to our legal counsel, Mr. Amos Cadbury."

"No need for that. My business concerns something that happened twenty-two years ago."

Marjorie looked relieved. She led him into a small room. "Twenty-two years ago."

"Obviously, you wouldn't have been working here then."

"Hardly."

Tuttle spelled out the problem for her algebraically, using no names. She followed what he said with a stern expression. Before he was well into his tale, she was shaking her head.

"We don't give out that kind of information."

"Would you stand in the way of that woman coming into a fortune?"

The question suggested that some fortune was in the offing, but Tuttle could not be responsible for how she interpreted his words. When they sank in, Marjorie's manner softened. She looked at his card and then at him, almost kindly. "I still think you should see Mr. Cadbury."

"Good idea." He took his card from her and returned it to his hat. "I just thought we could speed up matters. I only hope the delay has no negative effect on her chances."

"I can't do it, even if I could. It's a matter of ethics."

"I understand."

"See Mr. Cadbury."

Outside in his car, Tuttle thought. He had only the vaguest idea of the procedure for an adoption. He would have to pick someone's brains. He thought of the girl Hazel sometimes employed to gather materials, a paralegal by training. He searched for and found the odious cell phone. The second bit of luck came when he had turned it on and dialed his office.

"I've made an appointment for you," Hazel said without preamble. There was something like excitement in her voice.

"You know I'm busy."

"Not too busy for this."

"While I've got you, Hazel, get in touch with whatshername, the paralegal. I want everything on adoptions."

"Okay, okay. But listen."

He was to meet a young man in the Loop, in Water Tower Place, at the top of the escalator. "Bernard Casey." Hazel inhaled. "The way he talked, I looked him up. There is a Bernard Casey at Foley, Farnum, and Casey on Madison."

From the legal lowlands where he dwelt, Tuttle had often considered the great names in the law who practiced in the Chicago area. Foley, Farnum, and Casey represented an alpine peak. Hazel's excitement communicated itself to him.

"How will I know him?"

"He will know you. I mentioned your tweed hat."

"I'll be there."

Parking in the Loop meant two possibilities, either parking in the street and risking being towed away or putting his car in a garage and coming up with what would have been a down payment on its replacement. It was with the sense that his fortunes were turning that Tuttle nosed his car into a garage and then had to rise level after level until he was on the one called Ireland. The seventh level. Seven was his lucky number. It had taken him that many years to get through law school. He wedged his car into a narrow space, got out, pulled his tweed hat firmly onto his head, and went down in the elevator to the street.

He was two blocks from the Water Tower, the landmark that gave its name to the huge edifice across Michigan Avenue from it. With his topcoat flapping, Tuttle negotiated the traffic, weaving among the maniacal drivers and then given interference by a city bus. Through the revolving doors and up the escalator he went, craning his neck as if to make his tweed hat more visible. No one awaited him at the top.

He paced; he removed his tweed hat and put it on again; he paced some more. The thought grew on him that someone had used Hazel to play a practical joke. Was it possible that Hazel herself . . . He had pulled out his cell phone and switched it on when someone spoke.

"Mr. Tuttle?"

Tuttle whirled, his hand on the brim of his hat.

"Bernard Casey." He put out his hand. Tuttle took it. The young man exuded success. The dark suit must have cost five hundred dollars; his tie was richly tasteful. His expression became dubious, but then he overcame his doubts and suggested they have coffee.

Casey brought their cups to the table where he had ensconced Tuttle and lifted his in a toast. Tuttle sipped, scalding his mouth. He cried out.

"I'll get some water."

"It's okay," Tuttle managed to say.

"I should have warned you."

"Maybe I can sue."

Laughter. Casey brought up the suit against McDonald's some years before. Hot coffee had turned out to be against the law. This broke the ice.

"You practice in Fox River."

Tuttle nodded. Casey would have had to know this to contact his office.

"I apologize for not coming to you, Tuttle. I should tell you that I am a lawyer myself. What I need done has to be done in Fox River. It would be impractical to send one of our people out there." He paused. "No. Truth time. What I want to find out is for a friend of mine." Casey sipped his coffee with care. "Have you had anything to do with adoptions?"

"As a matter of fact, I have." Tuttle crossed his legs instead of his fingers.

"Good. I'll try to make this as concise as I can."

There was a young lady who had been adopted. She had been born in Fox River and given up to her foster parents at birth. She wanted to find her real mother.

"Of course, the mother may no longer be alive. She may long since have moved out of the area. If she married, who knows what her name might be?"

Tuttle lifted a hand. "Just leave all that to me. Your friend's name?"

"Martha Lynch."

Tuttle's heart leapt. Somewhere in the next world, his father must be guiding events. Through Martin Sisk, the Lynches had hired him to locate the mother of their adopted daughter. Now Bernard Casey, acting for the daughter, was asking him to do the same thing.

"I'll get at it." He hesitated. Bernard Casey drew a wallet from his inner pocket and put a hundred-dollar bill on the circular table. Tuttle covered it with one hand and shook Bernard Casey's with the other.

153

"I suppose it's all on record."

The image of the Fox River courthouse loomed in Tuttle's mind, the scene of so many of his defeats and his few small triumphs. He wished he had thought of that earlier. They exchanged cards, Casey somewhat surprised to see Tuttle's emerge from his tweed hat. He was glad he had retrieved it from Marjorie. It occurred to him that he could soon afford to have a new batch printed.

"I'll want all this to be just between the two of us," Casey said.

"Of course."

Casey had the look of a man who had accomplished his mission. "Do you know Amos Cadbury?"

"Everyone knows Amos Cadbury," Tuttle said carefully.

They parted there with another handshake. Tuttle eschewed the escalator and bounced down the stairs to the street. He had half a mind to call Hazel, but it was a thought easily rejected. At the garage, he ransomed his car with a credit card, but his manner was insouciant. Soon all his bills would be paid.

15

When Father Dowling mentioned the death of Nathaniel Fleck to Phil Keegan, Keegan said he would have Cy Horvath drop by the rectory. "I told you it wasn't exactly what we thought it was."

"What exactly was it?"

"Let Cy explain."

Since talking with Amos, Father Dowling had pondered the lawyer's normal dilemma. Madeline Lorenzo, the adoption of whose out-of-wedlock baby Amos had handled years before, had appeared in his office greatly upset by the reappearance of that child's father, who had abandoned her when she found she was pregnant. A familiar story, alas, the male refusing responsibility for his deed while the poor woman carried within her the result of their liaison. How many men had walked away from such a situation and thought of it no more. That Nathaniel Fleck, however belatedly, had felt the pangs of conscience was commendable, but his reappearance threatened the life that the mother had since built; she had a husband, a professor at Northwestern, and four children born of their union. A sense of responsibility that would have been welcome to her long ago had become a menace, and clearly Amos feared that she had been tempted to remove the threat to her marriage.

When Cy arrived, Marie showed him in. Father Dowling, feeling somewhat duplicitous, told the stolid Hungarian that he found himself still wondering about that strange event of the death of Nathaniel Fleck.

"I'll tell you what we know, Father."

Father Dowling had had many occasions for understanding the confidence Phil Keegan had in Horvath, assuring the pastor of St. Hilary's that Cy was worth half a dozen of his other detectives — "meaning the rest of the department." Cy still had the look of the football player he had been before an injury his freshman year at Illinois had sidelined him for good. In the service, he had been an MP; when he was discharged, he applied for the Fox River police. Phil had recognized the name from Cy's stellar career as a high school player and would have hired him on that basis alone. That Cy had turned into such an excellent detective was frosting on the cake.

Cy's description of the way the accident had altered from hit-and-run to something more ambiguous was familiar ground to Father Dowling. Having summed that up, Cy looked at the priest. "Of course, I wondered what he was doing in Fox River. He lived in California. There was a memorial service, you know."

"I heard."

"I went. Nothing said there explained why he was in the Chicago area, let alone Fox River."

"I suppose there could be a hundred explanations."

"One of them I found out. He had been at the alumni center at Northwestern — he was an alumnus — asking about a former classmate."

"Did he find him?"

"Her. I figured that, if he looked her up, she might know what he was doing here. Maybe she was the reason."

"Ah."

"Men get into their forties, they remember past loves. Maybe that was it, and he just wanted to see what the woman looked like now."

"So you were able to identify her."

"She's married to a faculty member at Northwestern. Mark Lorenzo."

"Did you talk to her?"

Cy shook his head. "Maybe I should have. But I talked to the husband. His office reminded me of this room."

"How so?"

"The books. Maybe more than you have."

"Well, after all, a professor. And what did you learn?"

"Fleck had got in touch with her, and she hadn't liked it at all. She refused to talk to him. Then he wrote her a letter. It looks as if he wasn't going to take no for an answer."

"What was the question?"

Cy shrugged. "As I said, men in their forties get romantic. Maybe he thought things could be as they had been."

"And she didn't."

"You can see how that got my mind going. Here's a man who shows up after all these years to see a happily married woman and makes a pest of himself. She panics. He is a threat. Then someone jumps a curb and he dives through a window and ends up dead. Naturally, I wondered who was driving that car."

"I can see that."

"Well, it couldn't have been her. Or him, for that matter. Their car couldn't be more different from the one the witnesses described."

"You checked it out?"

"Their car is a little compact. The vehicle that jumped the curb was an SUV. The Lorenzos have only the one car and don't use it much. Their life is pretty much lived on campus, and they can walk everywhere."

"Case closed?"

"As much as most of them are. We still have a man dead after a strange incident."

"But the Lorenzos no longer figure in it?"

"If they do, I'd like to know how."

Father Dowling felt vicarious relief for Amos Cadbury. Cy Horvath's account of his investigation would, when he heard it, take a great weight off the lawyer's mind. However, as Cy had indicated, that left a mysterious death mysterious still. When he was once again alone in his study, Father Dowling pondered the strange death of Nathaniel Fleck. There was, he persisted in thinking, something right about the man's desire to learn of the child he had fathered so long ago. That his curiosity had meant a great threat to the mother was also right. After all, the woman had resisted what must have been a great temptation simply to rid herself of the result of her folly. She had the child; it had been given up for adoption and, most fortunately, had been raised by the Lynches. Their reaction to their adopted daughter's curiosity about her real mother was also understandable, but who could not sympathize with the young woman's desire to know her true origins? Like most human affairs, this one was complex, the collision of intentions each of which had merit but which collectively had the great inconvenience of being irreconcilable. His own immediate reaction was relief that Amos's fears had no foundation. Thank God for Cy Horvath.

16

The realization that Mark had known her secret all along and had honored it made Madeline love her husband all the more. But how could she not feel rage at learning that it was her supposed dear friend Catherine Adams who had told him? What an odd sense that gave her in retrospect of the years of her marriage. All her memories of Catherine had been of her dearest friend, the one who had stood by her at the worst moment of her life. She remembered when she had returned stunned from the meeting when Nathaniel had made it clear that she was on her own.

"Thank God for *Roe v. Wade*," Catherine said.

"What do you mean?"

"There is a remedy, after all."

"No. No, I could never do that."

"Just think about it, Madeline. You'll see it's the only way."

The more she thought of it, though, the surer she was that she could never get rid of her baby like that. Catherine had supported

the decision she did not understand, helping Madeline deceive her parents, even sitting in on courses for her so that Madeline
earned credits she didn't deserve. An A- in
Latin! The following semester, she had
signed up for a course in Caesar and Cicero,
scrambling to learn the grammar she supposedly already knew — and got an A.

"Of course," Catherine had said. "You're
Catholic."

"Do you imagine we go to confession in
Latin?"

"Confession! Do you do that?"

"Only in English."

Several months before she gave birth, she
confessed her sins, prepared to be scolded
and treated like a scarlet woman, but when
the priest asked if she would have her child
and she said yes, he ended by congratulating
her. She emerged from the confessional
with the feeling that she had used her sin in
a bid for praise. In truth she was delighted
with herself that she had found the courage
to carry her child to term. Of course, the
Women's Care Center had been wonderful,
and when she met the woman who would
have her baby, any doubt she had had about
the wisdom of her decision was gone.

She had learned their name — not from
the center; they would never have told her,

and Madeline understood the policy. She was agreeing to let her baby go and had to put aside forever any thought of a reunion. It was quite by accident that she found it out. She volunteered each week at the hospital where she had delivered, with some vague thought that she was paying a debt, and one night she caught a glimpse of one of the doctors who had been there before she was put under and wheeled into the delivery room. She told herself that she would work up the courage to ask him, but she could never figure out what she would say that would lead him to tell her what she wanted to know.

"Oh, it's a medical family," someone said. "Lynch the pathologist is his son-in-law."

She kept an eye out for Dr. Lynch and was surprised to learn that he, too, had been there when she had her baby. They were in the phone book, and she drove past their suburban house, again and again, and at last she saw in the driveway the woman with whom she had wept. Then she knew. And that had been enough.

After she married Mark and had his children, one after the other, thoughts of her first baby dimmed. It would have seemed disloyal to remain curious about the child the Lynches had adopted. Then one day a few years ago, she had seen the photograph of Martha Lynch in the paper, salutatorian of her class at Barat College. The picture might have been her own graduation photograph. Rather than stirring up her desire to see her daughter, that photograph put an end to it. Everything had turned out all right, and it would be criminal to disturb the life her daughter had. Then the Monster had appeared.

Appeared and then almost immediately was struck down on a Fox River street. His death enabled her to think of him almost as she first had. His reappearance, now that it was no longer threatening, had a redeeming quality. Perhaps he had imagined that she had remained unchanged, that he could return and they could reclaim their child, and what had not been would be. But if her thoughts toward Nathaniel softened, those toward Catherine hardened into something very much like hatred, the hatred of the betrayed. Nathaniel had been weak, but what excuse did Catherine have for telling her secret to Mark? Talking with Janet and learning the extent of Catherine's perfidy filled her with loathing for the woman she had considered her best friend. Beware of best friends indeed.

Listening to Catherine at the memorial

for Nathaniel, astounded to hear her speak of her lifelong relationship with him, Madeline had been numbed, but her confusion became clarity when she went home and Mark told her he had always known her secret — had known, and it didn't matter. Clearly, Catherine must have imagined that telling him would abort their marriage.

She had not wanted to talk to Catherine at the memorial, but in the following days she became determined to confront her. There had been mention of the Hyatt Regency Chicago in one of the newspaper accounts, and Madeline phoned the hotel to find that Catherine Adams was still registered there. She took the train to the Loop.

She was told at the desk that Catherine's room did not answer. She felt frustrated. She descended to the street floor and sat in a chair and looked out at the urban scene, at the comings and goings of people, the revolving doors seemingly never still. Outside, taxis discharged their fares and valets took charge of vehicles.

Then she saw Catherine. She had just stepped out of a car and turned it over to a valet. Madeline watched her come through the doors and take the escalator, looking out over the open restaurant below as she was carried upward. After ten minutes, Madeline went to a house phone and asked for Catherine's room.

The length or brevity of time is contingent on our moods. Madeline seemed to wait forever while the phone rang in Catherine's room, yet during that time she hardly breathed.

"Yes?"

"Catherine?"

"Who is it?"

"Madeline."

The slightest of pauses and then a squeal. "Madeline, where are you?"

"In the lobby."

"Here in the hotel?"

"Yes."

"I'll be right down. My God. This is marvelous. Will I know you?"

"I'll know you."

Five minutes later, she appeared, descending on the escalator, looking expectantly at the scene below. Madeline awaited her at the foot of the escalator. Catherine took one look and came running into her arms.

"Oh, what a wonderful surprise. Madeline, you look wonderful."

"You've cut your hair."

"Only on the ends. Come, let's have a drink."

In the bar they ordered glasses of wine; Catherine charged them to her room. The place was full of people, mostly men in suits, the women elegantly dressed. Madeline felt frumpy in her faculty wife clothes. Catherine lifted her glass, looking at Madeline with a huge smile. Suddenly she leaned forward and kissed Madeline on the cheek.

"Don't even say how many years it's been. Tell me all about you."

"You were there at my wedding, remember."

"Of course I remember. And how is Professor Lorenzo?"

"I came to the memorial for Nathaniel. You were in our neighborhood."

"And it didn't even occur to me!"

"So you and Nathaniel became permanent."

"In a California way. Madeline, you're not jealous."

"Of a dead man?"

"Ouch." Her expression became the funereal one of the memorial. "I am determined that it won't destroy me. This is the most difficult thing I have ever lived through. A little secret. The last time I was with him, we quarreled. Not unusual, that. Ours was a lengthy quarrel punctuated by, well, you know. Still, it hurts to know that the last things I said to him were in anger."

"He came to see me."

Catherine put down her glass. "I know. That's what we quarreled about. I tried to stop him. It was crazy."

"Yes, it was."

"What did you tell him?"

"Tell him? I refused even to talk to him."

"Good for you. Imagine, after all these years, feeling the call of duty." She sipped her wine. "Of course, all writers are insane."

The longer they talked, the more disarmed Madeline felt. She had come determined to tell Catherine what a hateful person she was, what an awful thing it was to tell her secret to Mark in what had to be an effort to break them up. What could possibly drive this woman? But as they talked, as Catherine talked, glib, flowing, hardly needing to take a breath, Madeline felt her hatred ebb. The woman across from her was hollow, artificial, all surface. Any soul she had seemed to have seeped away, and she was reduced to chatter.

"Do you have children?"

"Four sons."

"My God. Well, he had hairy arms and a thick beard, it figures."

"Is that what does it?"

"Nathaniel hadn't a hair on his chest. And he was balding, in a nice way."

"So no children."

"Oh, that was never in the cards."

"Why did you tell Mark?"

Catherine seemed genuinely confused by the question. "Tell Mark what?"

Was it possible that what loomed so large for Madeline was insignificant to Catherine? She changed the subject. "Janet was at the memorial, too. You remember Janet. We talked afterward."

"And didn't come talk to me?"

"We didn't want to barge in."

"Oh, you. My best friend." Catherine put her head to one side and smiled. "If I kissed you again I would probably get arrested." She made a little face and shrugged. "So consider yourself kissed again. Madeline, why don't the three of us get together, you and I and Janet."

"How long are you in town?"

Catherine's face fell. "Oh my God, that's right. I'm flying back tonight. On the red-eye."

"Well, that's that."

"At least I've seen you."

It was forty-five minutes later that Madeline left. Catherine did kiss her again, in the lobby, and Madeline kissed her back.

169

Somehow the rage with which she had come downtown seemed uncalled for. Catherine in person did not inspire deep emotions.

17

Peanuts brought Tuttle the report Cy Horvath had written on his investigation of the downtown hit-and-run or whatever it was. At any other time, Tuttle would have read it immediately, but now, with several fish to fry, he just put it in his pocket. "Good work."

"You owe me a lunch."

Why not? Tuttle had spent the morning in old family court records, wasting hours until it occurred to him that Amos Cadbury was the key to his research. That required a competence with the computer Tuttle did not have. He called Hazel and had her put the paralegal on it.

"Just have her pull up everything twenty-two years ago that involved Amos Cadbury."

"What did Bernard Casey want?"

"I'd rather not say over the phone."

"So get back here and tell me."

"I should be there by midafternoon."

He waited for the sound of the phone being slammed down, but there was only an annoyed humming, and then that stopped. "Tell me about Martin Sisk."

"This afternoon."

She did slam down the phone then. Well, later he could divert her with stories of Martin and avoid telling her about the meeting with Bernard Casey. Meanwhile, he headed for the Great Wall with Peanuts.

"The law is endlessly interesting, Peanuts," he said through a mouthful of fried rice.

Peanuts grunted.

"Routine is the key," Tuttle continued. "And records. Records last, that is the point. Everything is filed away somewhere, and it is just a matter of finding it."

Peanuts hailed the waiter and ordered another beer. "You want that egg roll?"

"Take it."

Peanuts took it and made it disappear as if by a magician's trick. There were those who left Chinese restaurants with styrofoam boxes filled with what they had been unable to eat while there. Peanuts would never need a styrofoam box. His stomach was a styrofoam box. Tuttle looked at his mute friend with fondness. The report he had put in his pocket crinkled when he moved his arm. He got it out and began to read it. Peanuts, of course, went on eating. As he read,

Tuttle became suffused with an unfamiliar emotion. The parlay of Martin and Bernard Casey was already a sharp change in his fortunes — the daily double, as it were — but what he read in Horvath's report held the promise of a triple play. A hat trick. He took his tweed hat from the hook beside him and put it on.

Peanuts noticed. "You going?"

"Just my thinking cap." He hung it up again.

Peanuts was an ideal companion to ignore, and Tuttle let his thoughts run. The beauty of his situation was that he already knew what he had been hired to discover.

The Lynches, through Martin Sisk, wanted him to locate the natural mother of their adopted child. Bernard Casey wanted him to locate the natural mother of his friend Martha Lynch. Cy Horvath's report told him that Madeline Lorenzo was that mother. An inference, of course. Her panic at the reappearance of Nathaniel Fleck was due to the fact that he was the father of her illegitimate child.

Putting two and two together promised a set of fees that would bring a smile even to Hazel. He frowned. Such affluence might lessen her obvious intention of dealing herself into what she considered Martin Sisk's comfortable retirement. So what if he had twenty-five years on her. All the better, when you stopped to think of it.

The troubling element in all this was the death of Nathaniel Fleck. Cy Horvath all but conceded that it had been a freak accident, not a hit-and-run. Still, there had been a vehicle and the driver had sped away. Tuttle could not really believe that Horvath could dismiss that, but what could he do about it? The reports of the witnesses, as Cy had summarized them, were conflicting. No surprise there. The notion of an eyewitness is a fuzzy one when there are several witnesses and multiple pairs of eyes. The witnesses might have been describing different scenes.

When he and Peanuts finished at the Great Wall, Tuttle drove the replete little cop downtown. Only by talking with Horvath could he determine whether the detective had really closed the investigation. Meanwhile, the strange death of Nathaniel Fleck seemed a vague threat to Tuttle's impending triumph.

18

Janet called Madeline and suggested that they meet in a mall in Schaumburg.

"Our car is in the garage," Madeline said.

"Okay. Let's make it Evanston."

Any reluctance Madeline might have felt gave way to the prospect of telling Janet of her meeting with Catherine at the Hyatt Regency. She had decided not to mention it to Mark, before or after. What was the point? The past had put in an appearance and now would go away. Nathaniel was dead; Catherine had taken the red-eye back to California. Still, it would be good to talk to someone about it, and Janet was the obvious candidate.

They were hardly settled at a table with their coffee when Janet put a lurid publication on the table. "Have you seen this?"

"Good Lord, no." It was the sort of magazine that titillates shoppers as they wait at the checkout counter in supermarkets. Madeline had never seen anyone buy one, though everybody scanned them passing by.

"Look at this," Janet said. She opened

and folded the publication.

The photograph that appeared on the dust jackets of Nathaniel Fleck's books looked up at Madeline. In the simplest inflammatory prose the accompanying story mocked the claim of Catherine Adams to have been the companion of the dead author. Someone named Maurice Dolan, described as a golfing partner of Fleck, was quoted as saying that Fleck had dumped Catherine years ago. Again and again. "She wouldn't stay dumped." Janet's eyes were bright with malice.

"Well, well," Madeline said.

"Her performance at the memorial was a fraud."

"That isn't the most reliable kind of publication."

"I just know it's true."

Janet's attitude decided Madeline against mention of the meeting in the Hyatt Regency. Her own grievance against Catherine made the posthumous claim to being Nathaniel's lifelong companion, even if false, minor. Of course, there was irony in the possibility that a woman who had publicly insisted she made herself available to Nathaniel was lying. Most women would have lied to deny such a demeaning relationship.

"The poor thing."

"Well, you're certainly magnanimous about it."

"Janet, none of it matters anymore. It was all a long time ago. Now, thank God, it's over for good."

Janet thought about it. Clearly she was disappointed that the lurid story hadn't provided a basis for dismantling Catherine's character, but she closed the magazine and looked around for a wastebasket. When she had disposed of it, she sat again and gave Madeline a little smile. "I felt like an idiot when I bought that."

"Not much food for the mind."

"Now, tell me about your four sons."

It was like a return to normalcy, talking of her boys. Of course they were all brilliant, like their father. Stephen, the oldest, was a freshman at Northwestern.

"My daughter is a sophomore in high school. She's gone out for track."

It was that kind of conversation, listening to earn the right to talk, each of them eager to laud their offspring. Of course, with four sons, Madeline had an advantage.

"My youngest has asthma," she said.

"Ooooh."

"It can be controlled now, but it is a nuisance for him. Of course he's the athletic one."

After half an hour of such talk it seemed they really had very little in common anymore. Janet said she hadn't read a book in years. "And don't think it's because I read that kind of trash." She nodded toward the wastebasket.

Madeline tried to imagine a life without reading. Would that have become so important a part of her life if she hadn't married Mark? Perhaps not. But she had married him, and Janet's account of her husband's wheeling and dealing on behalf of Kraft Foods brought home to her what a wonderful life she had. Janet's remark that she supposed Madeline regretted not having at least one daughter made her uneasy, but it seemed to have no ulterior purpose.

"Maybe I still will."

And the two mothers laughed merrily.

Walking home, Madeline stopped at the supermarket and bought a copy of the publication Janet had shown her. Then she went to Mark's office. She dropped the paper on his desk.

"What's this?"

"Food for the mind."

"I think I already read this copy."

"Oh, sure. Look at this." She sought and found the story about Catherine.

When he had read it, he looked up. "Her checkered career continues."

Then she did tell him about meeting Catherine in the Loop. "I was going to tell her off. I went down there like an avenging angel. In the end, I just felt sorry for her."

"Good for you."

"Oh, pooh. Maybe I just lacked the guts."

He began to fold up the publication, then paused. "I wonder who Maurice Dolan is."

Madeline said nothing.

19

The news he had just received filled Amos Cadbury with dismay. Someone in records thought he would want to know that a request had been made for a list of all the cases in which Cadbury had been involved twenty-two years ago. Of course, all such records were in the public domain, available to anyone with the right to ask for them. The request had been made by Rebecca Young. The name meant nothing to Amos.

"She has paralegal training. She was acting for Tuttle."

Tuttle! A familiar melancholy settled over Amos Cadbury. For years he had tried to regard the ineffable Tuttle as an anomaly, a blemish on a noble profession, but the news of the day had long since deprived him of that delusion. After long decline, the law had entered a tragicomic phase. Professors wrote books in which they argued that the law was simply judicial interpretation, the supposed will of the people guiding the judge. All sense of self-evident truths backing up man-made law seemed to have gone. Everything was relative. What was just today might be the opposite tomorrow, should we, or those who presumed to speak for us, so decree. Things being that bad on the level of legal theory, who could wonder at the circus trials that dominated the news. Manifest killers were exonerated by juries who had been misled by the charlatans of criminal law. Each time a celebrity was accused of a crime, the same familiar faces appeared on television; sophists ready to prove that black is white and up is down would do anything inside and out of court to save their client, and this for fees that made Amos want to gag. In what the law had become, Tuttle seemed almost respectable, but his interest in Amos's cases of twenty-two years ago left little doubt in the lawyer's mind about what that interest was.

Much of Amos's waning legal career was spent on the estates of deceased clients, men and women whose wills he had written and whose intentions he was committed to seeing fulfilled. The younger men in the firm brought in new business; Amos was introduced ceremonially to new clients, the grand old man of the firm, but he had nothing to do with them. Over his long career he had been involved in many different sorts of problems, but he had handled only one adoption. Twenty-two years ago. The way he had handled it had been perfectly proper, but he had taken great pains to separate the parties in the matter. The release obtained from the young mother was conducted as a self-contained matter. The adoption papers, giving the Lynches possession of the child, had been filed in Indiana, in South Bend. Amos had done this personally, on an ostensible visit to his alma mater. He was confident that no one who came upon the one transaction could possibly be led to the other. Yet he was uneasy.

From Father Dowling he had learned that his awful suspicions concerning Madeline Lorenzo were unfounded. That left a mysterious death as mysterious as it had been, but sometimes an accident is one in the philosophical sense, unrelated to the intention of any agent, literally something that had happened but not been done.

"Thank God," Amos had said.

"Amen."

The question now was whether the care he had taken long ago could continue to protect his clients from heartbreak. Embarrassment and heartbreak were only inadequately prevented by the law, even by law at its best, and Amos had no doubt that he had acted for the best. Even Tuttle might sometimes succeed. Should the Lynches continue in their anxiety?

"Father, I wonder what would really be lost, after all these years, if the Lynches simply told their daughter of her origins."

"You wonder who they are really protecting."

"The mother has far more interest in maintaining the secret than they do."

"And what does she think?"

This was something only Amos could discover. He asked Madeline Lorenzo if she could come see him again.

When she came, Amos was once more struck by what a fine woman she was. Her youthful beauty had matured; there was about her an air of settled intelligence and the quiet authority of a parent. The thought that the wonderful life she had apparently fashioned with her husband should be jeopardized by a past in which she had acted so well made the old lawyer waver in his intention.

But it was she who broached the subject. "I have learned that my husband knew my secret all along."

"He did?"

"Before we married." She smiled a strange smile. "My best friend felt it her duty to tell him."

"Without effect?"

"He is a wonderful man."

"I don't doubt it. So it is no longer a secret."

"Not from him. But, of course, my children . . ."

"Ah. Of course."

"As you can imagine, I have been thinking a great deal of this lately. There is something you should know. The man I spoke to you about, the father, is dead."

"Nathaniel Fleck."

"You knew that?"

"That he was dead? The papers were full of it."

"That he was the father of my child."

"When we spoke before, if you should have asked me if I knew the man, I could quite honestly have said no. You mentioned receiving a letter from him. But then he wrote to me, too."

She looked at Amos for a time. "And you wondered if I had been responsible for his death?"

"My dear young lady."

"The police thought so. They had learned that Nathaniel Fleck had been to the alumni association at Northwestern, asking about me. That suggested a possibility they had to rule out."

"And, of course, did."

"They spoke to my husband. That is what prompted him to tell me that he had known all along of my baby by that man."

"Remarkable."

She smiled. "He is a philosopher."

"Even so."

She laughed a lovely laugh. "Oh, I will have to quote that to him."

"I have never aspired to amuse a philosopher."

"You have not said why you asked me to come."

"I, too, have thought much of these matters of late. The young woman, your daughter . . ."

There was a little catch of breath on Madeline's part, and then tears stood in her eyes.

"I understand that she wants to know. If there were some way we could meet and talk, maybe even get to know one another, it would be so wonderful. I long for that as much as she does, I think. But it is one thing for my husband to know and . . ." She sobbed.

"And another for your children."

She nodded, dabbing at her eyes. "I'm sorry."

Sorry that she wept at the thought of her

lost child? Certainly not that. Rather sorry that her long-ago misdeed had placed her in a dilemma in which, should she reveal herself to Martha, with all the delight that might bring, would also entail that her sons should learn something of which she continued to be ashamed.

"The problem now is that matters are not entirely in your hands."

"How so?"

"Your daughter is determined to find you. A lawyer is looking into the records of those events. What you understandably fear may come about by her doing."

She sat back. Her eyes went to the window. A series of emotions passed over her beautiful countenance. Amos Cadbury was seldom emotionally involved with those who came to him here; what they wanted was his mind and legal skills, not easy sympathy. But he felt his own heart ache for this young woman. He knew that long ago, when he talked to her in her distress and then presented her with the papers he had prepared, he was acting more on behalf of the Lynches than for her. At the time, he had seen what he was doing as a means of rescuing her from a grievous problem, but any future results he might have imagined would have concerned the family that adopted her child. Had he supposed that a mother could emerge wholly unscathed by what she had done, by what she was doing? Suddenly he had the most vivid memory of the way she had thanked him after she read and signed the papers, a lovely waif from whose shoulders he had lifted a burden. How could he have felt other than like her benefactor?

"I don't blame her," she said after a time. "In her circumstances, I would do the same thing."

"It is not an ignoble thing to want to know one's mother."

"You think she will succeed in finding me?"

"It is not impossible."

"I have seen her, you know."

"You have?"

"I should have mentioned this before. It happened quite by accident that I came to know who had adopted her. I had to see her. And I did. More than once. So you see, we are very much alike."

"You can just wait and see what happens."

"I couldn't decide otherwise now. The decision is not mine alone."

"I should tell you that the lawyer involved is not the most competent."

"Oh, I don't want it to happen like that, to be discovered like some kind of criminal."

"If she thought you were that, she would not want to find you."

"And the foster parents?"

"The wife is adamantly opposed. She sees this as a repudiation of all she has done for her daughter."

"She and I should meet."

Amos thought about it. Whatever happened, these two women, the mother and the foster mother, would be brought together.

"That may be a very good idea."

"Could you tell her?"

"I will make discreet inquiries."

She looked at him with wry affection. "You are such a nice man."

"Now, now."

They parted with the understanding that Amos would see if Sheila Lynch would want to talk with Madeline Lorenzo.

"We got along so well then, long ago," Madeline said.

He walked her to the door and watched her cross the reception area and leave. He said that he did not wish to be disturbed. Behind his closed office door, he sat at his desk and looked out the window, his eyes moist with tears.

20

Father Dowling had been pondering Amos's account of his visit with Madeline Lorenzo when he was suddenly called to the school. Grace Weaver had struck Martin Sisk with a pool cue, and Martin cowered in a corner while Grace threatened to beat him further. Edna Hospers finally took the cue from her, and all the ladies converged to hear what Grace's grievance was.

"That man is a beast!"

This increased the sisterly sympathy of her comforters. Martin drew no supporters but crept from the corner holding his elbow. "I think she's broken something."

"I hope so!" cried Grace.

That was when Edna called the rectory. One of her recurrent fears was that some accident or worse would occur at the center, and the parish would find itself in legal difficulties. Far-fetched, perhaps, but Father Dowling appreciated her concern and went to the school. Edna drew him aside and recounted the episode.

"Of course, the two of them have been an item, Father."

"I myself have seen them walking hand in hand."

At that point, Martin hurried up to Father Dowling. He looked at Edna. "Did you tell him what she did?"

"Her complaint is about what you did, Martin," Edna said, and left him with the pastor.

"Well, now," Father Dowling said.

"She struck me with a pool cue, swinging it like a bat. The thick end hit me."

"A lover's quarrel?"

A wonderful blush suffused Martin's cheeks. "Father, I am in my seventies."

"I sometimes wonder if anyone really feels the age he is."

"This is my arthritic elbow."

"Martin, why don't you make it up to her? It's the only way things will settle down."

"The woman is jealous."

"Good Lord, is there someone else?"

Again the blush. "She misunderstood me."

"Which she?"

But it accomplished nothing to tease Martin and make him more foolish than he had made himself. Father Dowling took his other elbow and led him toward the ladies, who parted like the Red Sea. Grace glared at Martin.

"Martin wants to apologize, Grace," Father Dowling said.

Martin got his elbow free. "Apologize for what?"

"For telling me of the young woman who is pursuing you!" Grace cried.

"Who?" asked a chorus of voices.

"Ask Romeo."

"I was joking," Martin cried.

"No, you weren't. I know when you're joking."

"Grace, please."

His pleading tone melted her. Her comforters urged her toward Martin. Fearful that a shotgun wedding was in the offing, Father Dowling headed for the door.

"Father?" It was Henry Dolan. "I'll walk back with you."

"Are you sure your medical attentions won't be needed?"

"My specialty was knocking people out."

"Grace is giving you competition."

They went outside and started up the walk toward the rectory.

"If you're free, I would like to continue the talk we had before."

"Of course."

Marie's welcome to Henry Dolan rivaled

that she gave Amos Cadbury. "Doctor! How are you?"

Father Dowling went on to the study, and in a moment Henry joined him. When the door was closed, he took a pipe from his pocket and showed it to Father Dowling.

"So you've taken up smoking again."

"No. I tried and found it was not at all as I had remembered. Smelling your pipe smoke filled me with memories of how pleasant it was to light up. I find it anything but." He dropped the pipe in the wastebasket. "Besides, I didn't like sneaking around so Vivian wouldn't notice."

"That is no way to smoke."

"We live in changing times."

"Alas."

"Do you remember what I came to you about, my daughter's adopted child?"

Amos Cadbury had told Father Dowling of his recent discussion with Madeline Lorenzo. Perhaps this was an opportunity to find out if objections on the side of the Lynches to Martha's curiosity were what they had been.

"Has anything changed?"

"My granddaughter is adamant."

"As you suggested, I talked with Amos Cadbury about it. I have just talked with him again. There are developments that you

192

should know of. It seems that a lawyer is looking into the matter of the adoption."

"On whose behalf?"

"Amos didn't know."

"Martha," Henry said softly. "The man she is in love with is a lawyer."

"If Amos is right, he would not be the lawyer. Does the name Tuttle mean anything to you?"

"Oh my God."

"It does?"

"This is Vivian's doing. She thinks the birth mother should be warned about Martha's curiosity. That idiot Martin Sisk offered to have inquiries made. I'm sure Tuttle is the lawyer he went to." He stopped. "Well, I won't go into our little domestic squabbles here. It's bad enough to talk of these family matters with someone else, but Martin Sisk!"

"Amos has spoken with the mother."

Henry stared at him and then began to dig in the wastebasket. He found his discarded pipe. "Can I have some tobacco?"

"Never smoke in anger, Henry."

"Oh, I suppose you're right. Maybe I thought I could punish Vivian by lighting up."

Father Dowling then relayed to Henry what Amos had told him. However incompetent Tuttle might be, there was the chance that he would succeed in unraveling the mystery. The birth mother was considering whether the time had come to lift the veil on the past.

"She doesn't want to be found out as if she were hiding," Father Dowling said.

"I guess I can understand that, but hiding is what we've all been doing."

"If Martha makes the discovery against everyone's wishes, things could be very difficult."

"A point I have tried to make to my daughter."

"Do you think you might make it again, in the light of these developments? I am relaying Amos Cadbury's wish."

Henry nodded, turning his pipe in his hands. "Sometimes I think we have made this far more of a problem than it is by thinking we could keep Martha from knowing. After all, what real difference could it make now?"

"The mother of the child faces far more of a real problem, Henry. Her husband, as it turns out, has known all along she had a baby before they married. That presented no impediment to him, and he has been silent all these years. Until recently. But there are her other children. She has four sons."

"Four."

"Amos tells me that she is a wonderful woman, a devoted wife and mother." He paused. "He says she is very much like Martha."

"It's cruel to keep this knowledge from Martha. If the mother is agreeable, I mean."

"She wanted time to think about it."

"I will see what I can do."

There was a rap on the door and Marie looked in, her expression one of wild anxiety. "Your wife is here. Something has happened."

Vivian Dolan hurried into the study and ran to her husband. "It's Maurice. Something has happened to him. You must go to him."

"What happened?"

"He collapsed on the golf course."

PART THREE

1

Vivian Dolan was too upset to go, and so Amos Cadbury did not hesitate to make the trip to California with Henry Dolan, a long flight in which his old friend could indulge his anxieties as they sat side by side in business class.

"We never once went out to visit the boy, Amos."

"You wouldn't have wanted him to think you were checking up on him."

Henry liked this explanation. "Of course, Vivian dreads flying, and it would have been a terribly long drive."

"Henry, he hasn't been there three years."

"Of course, he sent us photographs of the place, and we had your description too, Amos."

Better this kind of conversation than going over and over the enigmatic message that explained their flying west. All Henry knew was that his son had collapsed on the golf course and been taken to the hospital.

"He was never sick a day in his life."

Amos had asked for the name of the hospital and telephoned before leaving for home to get ready to go off with Henry. Maurice was in intensive care.

"What is the diagnosis?" Amos asked the doctor, after identifying himself as the family attorney.

"It's his back."

"His back."

He had almost decided to cancel the trip. He would have imagined heart, despite Maurice's relative youth, but his back? Well, Amos was no physician, and maybe a back can be that serious. Why else would Maurice be in intensive care?

Henry had not seemed overly relieved when Amos told him what the problem was. "Children are wonderful, Amos, but they never cease causing anxiety."

Inevitably they talked of poor Sheila and her adopted child. They were offered drinks by the flight attendant, and Henry asked for a single malt scotch, which he sipped neat. Amos was content with coffee.

"They are a blessing, Henry. Believe me."

Henry put a sympathetic hand on Amos's childless arm. "I know, I know."

"Did you speak to Sheila about meeting with Madeline Lorenzo?"

A painful look. "She wouldn't talk about it."

"It would be the sensible thing. Imagine what she will feel if Martha finds out by herself. I told you that a lawyer is looking into it."

"Tuttle!" It had suddenly occurred to Henry that the family secret might be in the public domain. Why did all of them, Henry and Vivian, Sheila and George, look on the adoption as somehow shameful? Well, not George. George had approached Amos at the University Club. He took a chair next to his in the library and sat silently for a time. George was a taciturn man, but he was a man of feeling, pathologist or not.

"Henry Dolan has been speaking to you, Amos," George had said.

"Yes."

"He speaks for us all, of course."

"Of course."

"You've talked with the mother, too."

"Several times."

"How is she?"

"Thriving. She has four sons."

"Four. Isn't that marvelous?"

"She has had some upsetting experiences of late."

After a moment of silence, George said, "The father?"

"Yes."

George shook his head. "I wish there were

201

something we could do for her. We owe her so much."

"She has offered to meet with Sheila."

A long silence, even for George. "Would she meet with me?"

"I could ask."

"Please do."

But before he had been able to follow through on George's suggestion, the frantic call from Henry had come, and here the two of them were sailing along at thirty-eight thousand feet toward California. Below, the moonscape of the western mountains changed colors in the sun. Amos was sure that George's suggestion was his own, that neither Sheila nor the Dolans knew of it. Henry had dozed off. Amos looked down at the changing landscape and thought of his late wife, gone now more than a dozen years, her memory still vivid. Sometimes, at night, he was awakened by the sound of her voice calling him and knew the disappointment that it was only a dream. Still, it was a consoling thought that she was looking after him. It was his deepest hope that they would once more be together, forever. Few who knew Amos would suspect him of sentimentality, but from time to time, late at night, while smoking his cigar and sipping brandy, he put on "Danny Boy" and submitted himself to its lachrymose sentiments. He himself often breathed an Ave for his departed wife, but it was the rising ending of the ballad that brought tears to his eyes. *You will bend and tell me that you love me, and I will rest in peace until you come to me.*

Henry slept on, and Amos, too, dozed off. They were awakened by the announcement that they had begun to descend for their approach into the airport known by the disconcerting acronym LAX. They landed and disembarked, and when they came out onto the street, there was the distinctive structure, looking like some long-legged insect. They took a taxi directly to the hospital.

Henry had taken the precaution of asking George to contact a Los Angeles colleague, and thus their way was smoothed. Forty-five minutes after landing, they were at Maurice's bedside. He lay on his stomach, so Henry pulled up a chair and sat, the better to speak to his son.

"Dad."

"How are you, son?"

"Why are you here?"

"More important, how are you feeling?"

"Very little at the moment. I warn you, I'm groggy."

Henry nodded. Doubtless he knew what pain relievers had been administered to

Maurice, Amos thought. "So what happened?"

Maurice, speaking with a thick tongue and slowly, described what had happened on the thirteenth fairway. "The thirteenth!" He smiled. "I had a helluva drive and took my second shot. It's a par five, and I wanted to make the green in two. I gave it all I had and, bam, my back gave out. You wouldn't believe the pain. I collapsed and then the lights went out. I came to in the ambulance."

Amos fought the feeling that he had come a long way for something less than an emergency.

Henry said, "I'll look at your chart. Amos will stay with you."

"Amos?" Maurice had been unaware of his presence. Amos felt like Colonel Brandon in *Sense and Sensibility* looking in as Marianne at last comes to. Maurice tried to look over his shoulder but groaned with the effort. Amos took Henry's place in the chair and faced Maurice. "You came all this way, Mr. Cadbury?"

"The message was alarming."

"Message. I didn't send any message."

"Didn't you give the hospital a name to be notified?"

"Not Dad's."

"It doesn't matter. We're here."

Henry looked in to say that he would be consulting with some of the staff. Amos waved him on his way.

Maurice talked in a dreamy way of many things. The driving range — he wanted Amos to see what a success it was. It seemed a better excuse for the trip than Maurice's ailment. "A secret, Amos. I met Martha's mother."

"You did!"

"A mutual friend put me onto it. As soon as I saw her I knew. The spitting image."

"Did you tell your sister?"

"Sheila? No. She treats it as a big secret."

"You must tell me about that meeting."

"Sure, sure." But the nurse came in and added something to the liquids that were dripping into Maurice, and he faded away. Amos was standing at the window when Henry returned.

"There has to be an operation. Disks. It can be very serious. I'm taking him home."

Making the arrangements took several days. Henry had to override the advice of colleagues, but he was adamant: He wanted his son back in Fox River. Meanwhile, they made a visit to the driving range. Balls were being hit with varying degrees of skill. The place was crowded; the shop in which equipment and food were sold was doing a brisk business. Everyone in charge was young, with bronzed skin and long hair. Amos would have thought them delinquents, but they were obviously efficient.

A woman came out of the office. She looked at the elderly gentlemen in suits and came to them. "Can I help you?"

Amos said, "You must be Catherine Adams."

Henry made the connection. The silent partner. "I am Maurice's father."

"He's not here. Have you heard?"

"We've just come from the hospital."

"Good, you do know. I'm looking after things a bit in his absence."

Her close-cut hair was oddly attractive, Amos thought. What a place California was. The men with hair to their tail bones and women in crew cuts. It was all perversely attractive. Perhaps that was the point.

"I'm taking him home for the operation."

"Operation?"

"It's quite serious. There is an excellent man in Fox River who will perform the surgery."

"We were both in Chicago a week ago."

"Maurice came to see me," Amos said.

She opened her mouth in feigned shock. "And didn't breathe a word. What a fox he is."

"So you're the silent partner," Henry said again. He seemed taken by Catherine Adams.

"I don't know about silent. Except legally." She smiled at Amos. "I should explain it to you."

Amos felt flirted with, too, and didn't mind a bit. They went into the office.

"Maurice's trophies," she said, gesturing at a set of glassed-in shelves. "I won't let him bronze me."

"Will everything run smoothly here with Maurice away?"

"It always does. He makes a courtesy appearance once a day, and then it's off to the golf course or wherever."

"And you?"

"Oh, don't worry about me. I'm used to being abandoned."

Henry clearly took her banter to mean that there was something between her and Maurice, and equally clearly he liked it.

"You could come along. I'm renting a plane."

"Renting a plane? That sounds like Rock Hudson. But I can't go with you, unfortunately."

"I'll keep you informed. How can I reach you?"

"Just call Maurice's number." She paused. "I'll check his messages."

Amos was reminded of the girl who had answered the door when Vivian called at Maurice's apartment on the North Side, but if Henry suspected anything he concealed it. Maybe he thought cohabitation would lead to something more. He seemed to be assessing Catherine Adams for childbearing possibilities.

The next day, the ambulance plane was ready. When Amos saw its size he declined Henry's offer of a ride, but he was there when Maurice, accompanied by a nurse, was brought from the hospital and put onto the plane. He said good-bye to Henry before the door was closed.

"What a good friend you are, Amos."

"Have a good flight."

He watched the little plane taxi away. He would be as likely to take a hang glider to Chicago as fly in such a plane as that. Who was Rock Hudson, he wondered, but not for long. Now that he was here, he planned to stay a few days longer in Los Angeles.

2

Knowledge is power, as someone has said. Tuttle never knew who, only that it was true. The question was what to do with it. The document releasing her baby that Madeline had signed had been turned up by his paralegal, but the adoption papers assigning the child were nowhere to be found. Not for the first time, Tuttle found himself admiring the skills of Amos Cadbury. The birth certificate only confirmed what the release revealed: A daughter had been born to a single mother, and that single mother had put her child up for adoption. There the trail ended. Tuttle discounted the possibility that the Lynches had no legal claim to their daughter. That the two children were the same was still an inference, and one Tuttle never doubted, but what good was a hunch, legally? Maybe if he had gone to a better law school, or done better at the one he had attended, he would know what to do next. He had no memory of any discussion of adoptions in any class. Had Amos studied adoptions in the Notre Dame law school? Then Tuttle had another hunch. Amos was doubtless a member of the Indiana bar. He had gone to school in South Bend. He would have lawyer friends there.

Tuttle hopped into his Toyota, risked the Skyway, as usual under repair, and set out on the Indiana Tollway for South Bend. Two hours after his arrival, he had found the Lynches' adoption papers.

Tuttle celebrated by driving out to Notre Dame, where he talked his way past the gate guard and toured the legendary campus. He lifted his tweed hat as he passed the grotto. Ducks waddled on the road, making the 20 mph speed limit seem unnecessary. A flock of Canada geese brought him to a standstill. Why did anyone go hungry when there was that much meat stopping traffic? Everyone complained about Canada geese, but no one did anything about them. Tuttle considered talking Tetzel, the reporter, into writing a piece for the *Fox River Tribune*. A modest proposal. Let them eat geese. He was feeling giddy with triumph. He came to another gate and exited the campus. If he were a drinking man, he would have toasted his success. Instead, he headed for the tollway and home.

Now he sat in his office, with the door closed, considering that knowledge is power. In the outer office, Hazel was banging things around, in a mood.

"Where have you been?" she had demanded when he sauntered in.

Tuttle looked around. "Martin here?"

"That dingbat."

"Trouble in paradise?"

"Some old woman called and told me to keep my hands off Martin Sisk."

"I would have thought the risk ran in the opposite direction."

"Tell me, Tuttle, what is he worth?"

"He's loaded. He ran a pharmacy across from the courthouse, did a land office business."

"So he tells me."

"It's true. You could do worse, Hazel."

"You're telling me."

The way she looked at him sent him swiftly into his office, shutting the door behind him. He did not take off his tweed hat. Well, just enough to look at it with awe. Between his father and his tweed hat, he felt he would remain on a lucky roll. But how should he use what he knew?

He could confront Amos Cadbury and congratulate him on the way he had handled the Lynch adoption. He let the imagined scene unroll behind twice-closed eyes — he had pulled his hat over his face — but not even in double darkness could he come up with an Amos Cadbury cowed by his discovery and anxious to take Tuttle into his confidence. He pushed back his hat and picked up the phone.

"Get me Martin Sisk."

"Are you serious?"

"Quite."

"Have you been drinking?"

"Only of your beauty, my dear." He had locked his door when he shut it.

"Ha." The sound in his ear altered, and he took the phone away. He could hear Hazel punching buttons in the outer office. He waited for her to tell him Martin was on the line, but what he heard was her voice, and not the voice with which she spoke to him. The delay was suddenly welcome. Obviously Hazel was making it up to Martin. He went to the door and tried to hear. She seemed to be teasing him about his girlfriends, the ones who called to threaten her, but her voice was sweet as honey. Tuttle returned to his chair. Martin didn't have a chance against Hazel. She would marry and quit, and he would have the office to himself again. Once more he and Peanuts could while away the hours, having

Chinese sent in, pigging out. The phone rang.

"Mr. Sisk."

"Thank you, Hazel. Martin?" He paused. "Hang up, Hazel."

A moment passed and she was off.

"Mission accomplished, Martin. Where can we meet?"

"Mission accomplished?"

"The mother of the adopted daughter," Tuttle said impatiently.

"Oh, yes. Of course. But haven't you heard?"

Tuttle felt a sinking sensation. "Heard what?"

"Let's put that on hold, okay? Vivian's son, Maurice, has been taken ill in California. Henry Dolan flew out there. This isn't the time."

"It is for us, Martin. Where are you?"

"I'll meet you," Martin said hastily. "Name a place. Not your office."

"The Great Wall. On Dirksen. In half an hour."

He hung up. What did Vivian's son have to do with it? In any case, delay seemed dangerous. He unlocked his door and emerged into the outer office.

"Is he coming here?"

"He's shy, Hazel. But he's hooked."

"What did he say?"

"He doesn't trust himself in your presence."

"Get out of here."

Tuttle got out of there.

3

"Any word?" Martha asked Bernard.

"These things can take time."

He had come to her desk. Willa looked on with approval over a file cabinet. Bernard turned, and Willa disappeared.

"How about a drink after work?"

She nodded.

"And then dinner."

She loved him so much, even when he didn't look at her that way.

"I'll ask my boss."

"I'm your boss."

After work they came out of the building and headed into the wind. Tonight would be Italian. "With Chianti. To weaken your resistance."

He was kidding. They loved one another but were keeping things under control. It was the Catholic way. At least it should be. At Gregorio's they began with canneloni and went on to veal. The Chianti was heady, and she resolved to sip.

"I've had a great idea," he said.

"Tell me."

"While we're waiting, we get the ball rolling. What's your parish?"

"My parish?"

"Look, we're going to have to endure pre-marital instruction. God only knows how long that may take. So we talk to your pastor, tell him our intentions, and get under way."

She found it exciting. Why not? If she found out, when she found out, she wouldn't have changed. Of course she would marry Bernard in any case, barring some awful revelation. But not in the Loop church she attended.

"I want to be married where my parents and grandparents were. St. Hilary's in Fox River."

"But you don't live in Fox River."

"My parents do."

"Good enough. Fox River it is."

"St. Hilary's."

He lifted his glass and she lifted hers. Then he brought out the ring.

"Oh, Bernard."

He slipped the ring onto her finger — a perfect fit — and then he came around and kissed her. Other diners applauded when she hung out her left hand in explanation. Bernard took her home and she asked him in, and it was all they could do to keep their love in its prenuptial phase. She scrambled off the couch.

"I'll make coffee."

"At this hour?"

"A beer?"

"Ugh."

So they sat drinking ice water, just looking at one another. Finally, he asked her to get out the phone book, and they looked up St. Hilary's. He jotted down the number.

"Of course we'll go together."

"We do, don't we?"

For a while, it seemed that not even ice water could cool his ardor, but in the end virtue emerged, if not entirely unscathed, still victorious. The next day came the awful news about Uncle Maurice.

Her grandmother didn't make much sense when she called Martha at the office, and it was difficult to discover what exactly had happened, but her grandfather was flying to his son's side. Vivian was obviously in no condition to go.

Maurice was the one person she felt really related to, no matter that she was adopted. He was the black sheep, a notorious disappointment, though in the past few years he seemed to have redeemed himself in California. Martha called Sheila to get a more coherent report.

"He collapsed on the golf course."

"Oh my God. His heart?"

"We're waiting for Grandpa to call. Amos Cadbury flew out with him."

Amos Cadbury, the pillar of strength. Of course he would accompany his old friend Henry Dolan. Perhaps he thought of Grandpa as his young friend. Whenever the family faced a crisis, Amos Cadbury was at their disposal. It was he who had gone to California a few years ago to oversee Maurice's entry into the driving range business, which seemed tailor-made for her vacillating uncle. Anything connected with golf was Maurice's cup of tea. It had seemed the perfect solution, and apparently had been. At noon, Martha went up the street to St. Peter's and prayed for Maurice. Tears came at the thought that she might never see him again, that what had happened to him would prove fatal. She lit a candle for him before the statue of St. Anthony of Padua.

That afternoon, Bernard came in. "I looked for you at noon."

She told him about Maurice and how she had spent her noon hour. He put his hand on her shoulder. Across the office, Willa turned discreetly away.

That morning, Martha had not mentioned her new ring, but it seemed to announce its own presence, glittering on her hand. Willa had finally noticed it. Her squeal had brought everyone around Martha. The newest paralegal asked who the lucky man was, and the others laughed.

"Bernard Casey, my dear," Willa said. Her manner might have suggested that she had arranged the match.

The call bringing the news about Maurice cut into this triumphant conclave.

Now Bernard said, "I called St. Hilary's and spoke with Father Dowling. Saturday morning at ten."

4

Martin Sisk had convinced Grace Weaver that Hazel meant nothing to him, wondering how she had learned of the evening he and Hazel had spent watching *From Here to Eternity* at his place. The truth was he was almost frightened of the predatory Hazel. During the beach scene, while Burt and Deborah tumbled in the surf, she put her hand on his knee as she leaned against him. Her breathing had become heavier.

"My wife hated this movie," Martin said, his voice high and nervous. Hazel ignored the remark. Her hand moved, though her eyes remained on the screen.

She grunted approvingly when the stabbed Ernest Borgnine, the beast who had beaten Frankie, fell dead of the wounds inflicted by Montgomery Clift. She wept openly when Clift played "Taps" for Frankie. She had slid down a bit on the couch, to equalize their heights, and now she lifted her face to his. Martin patted her cheek and leapt from the couch and began to fuss with the VCR. He was assailed by two thoughts. One, that Hazel would offer little resistance if he returned to the couch; indeed, she would be the aggressor. The second thought was that it would be a deed from which he could never step back. It was one thing to flutter and flirt, to engage in amorous banter, but to go for the big enchilada was a possibility that had ever lain over the horizon of his mind.

He escaped. They finished the popcorn. He had turned on all the lights in the living room. Hazel followed his movements as a cat follows a mouse. The important thing was not to rejoin her on the couch. And he didn't. He yawned, faking it at first, but then it became real.

"You're right," she said. "You'd better take me home."

When he had, he opened the passenger door for her to get out and said good night to her on the curb.

She smiled and patted his cheek. "You are a gentleman."

The gentleman watched her go to her door unaccompanied. When he drove away he felt as Adam might have if he had refused the apple.

But they had been observed. Two days later, Grace confronted him. He tried to lie, but he had never been good at lying. Grace hit him with a pool cue, and after the ensuing public disgrace, they reconciled. They went for a walk, going back and forth between the school and rectory, where he dismissed Hazel. He explained how he had met her.

"What were you doing in a lawyer's office?"

"My financial affairs are complicated. Secure, but complicated."

"What's the lawyer's name?" Her tone was skeptical.

"Tuttle."

He thought of telling Grace exactly how he had fought off the secretary's advances, but good sense prevailed.

All was peace again, until Hazel called to say that Tuttle wanted to see him. Before she put him through, she told him of Grace's call. Martin wished that he had not given Grace the name of the lawyer.

"Aren't you the busy bee? I had no idea I was being recruited for a harem."

It was good to be restored to the role of Lothario when no immediate danger threatened. Still, he had sense enough to insist that Tuttle meet him at a neutral site.

"I've never been here before," he said when he found Tuttle in a booth at the Great Wall.

"I can't tell you how much business I've conducted right here. Take a pew."

Tuttle used again the phrase he had used on the phone, "Mission accomplished." He had found the mother of Martha Lynch.

"How did you do it?"

Tuttle held up a hand, his expression suggesting arcane knowledge beyond Martin's capacity for understanding.

"More important, who is she?"

Tuttle adopted a serious expression. "Martin, we have reached a point when I have to know why you want this information. I cannot be party to disturbing the peace and tranquility of innocent lives. There has to be a reason why it was so difficult for me to dig up this information."

"I told you. Vivian Dolan wants to know."

"Am I to be her lawyer or yours?"

"She doesn't even know I've come to you. I'm doing this as a favor."

Tuttle sat back and adjusted his absurd tweed hat. "That puts a very different complexion on it."

"What are you talking about? I'm your client. I gave you twenty dollars."

For answer, Tuttle got out his wallet and put it on the table. He did not open it.

"And I signed all those papers with your secretary."

"Ah, Hazel. You have made a conquest there, Martin."

Good God, had she told Tuttle about *From Here to Eternity*? Martin managed not to blush, but he was uneasy.

"Tell me who the woman is."

"Knowledge is power, Martin, as the poet says. How do I know how you would use the information if I told you?"

"I would pass it on to Vivian Dolan. Period."

Tuttle nodded. "In that case, I think I will eliminate the middle man." He opened his wallet and took out five dollars. He pushed the bill toward Martin.

"But I gave you twenty."

"Chalk it up to expenses. The main thing is, this concludes our professional relationship."

Martin was furious. He refused the offer to have lunch, no matter how good Tuttle claimed the sweet and sour chicken was at the Great Wall. He felt that he had delivered Vivian to the male counterpart of the predatory Hazel.

For all that, he wanted credit for the effort he had made on Vivian's behalf. And he might warn her about Tuttle. Too late, he was remembering the little lawyer's reputation around the courthouse. He decided that he would pass on the good news to Vivian, but when he called, she was almost hysterical. Something dreadful had happened to her son, Maurice, in California. Henry had flown there, accompanied by Amos Cadbury. Martin offered to come sit with her, but she seemed not to understand. So he went walking with Grace and told her about poor Maurice Dolan.

"That boy was always such a trial to them," Grace said.

"How are your children, Grace?"

"Scattered to the four winds, absorbed in their families, as they ought to be. I am as alone as I was before I married."

Her arm was warm against his side. The incident with the pool cue was forgotten. One thing about Grace, if they danced she would let him lead.

5

Once it had been simply St. Joseph's Hospital; now it was the St. Joseph Medical Center of Fox River. Its management had passed from the nuns to a national organization adept in the manipulation of insurance claims and government grants. Henry Dolan was glad he had been born when he had been. The hospital, which had once been as familiar to him as the back of his hand, now with additions and rearrangements had altered almost beyond recognition. He began to wonder why he had brought Maurice all the way from California to this impersonal place. But then Dr. Wippel swept into the room, and soon he and Henry were in close consultation. Other old colleagues joined them. The charts Henry had brought from California were studied. Then Wippel went in to examine his patient.

The next few hours were satisfyingly busy. Maurice was put through an MRI; lab tests were hurried to completion. Afterward, first to Henry in the hall, and then next to the bed so Maurice could understand what lay ahead, Wippel outlined what he would do.

"The back is a delicate mechanism," he began. He had a series of illustrations in different colors, displaying the delicate intricacy of the human back. His buffed nail pointed to the lower spine. "The problem is there." He gave Maurice a somewhat less graphic description of the operation than he had given Henry in the hall.

"And that will take care of it?" Maurice asked. He had been following the explanation attentively.

"There is less than a five percent chance of failure."

"But will I be able to golf again?"

Wippel answered reassuringly.

Vivian came in. It was the first time she had seen her son since Henry had brought him back. She seemed surprised at Maurice's alertness. Her weeping was under control.

"Don't worry, Mom. They say I'll be able to golf."

"Oh, Maurice." She tried to take him in his arms, but Wippel eased her away. Henry gave his son a reassuring look and led Vivian out.

There was no need to go into the gory details with Vivian. Wippel said a few words to her and went off to prepare. Henry had decided that he would stay away from the OR. The fact was, he had been a little unnerved by Wippel's explanation. He had reduced the chance of failure to five percent, but that didn't eliminate the possibility that Maurice might come out of this permanently handicapped. How altogether typical of Maurice to wonder if he would be able to golf again. What would life mean to him if he were kept off the golf course?

Wippel operated on Maurice the morning after the young man was admitted to the hospital. Both Henry and George experienced the anxiety, unfamiliar to them, of those waiting for news of a loved one. Vivian sat staring at a huge photograph of a Japanese garden, doubtless chosen to induce tranquility. It seemed to be working. Vivian had finally got herself under control. The alarming news had unleashed all the years of worrying and fretting about Maurice, but now, with the operation under way, she sat staring at the picture. Sheila seemed unable to sit. Henry took her outside.

"Has Martha been told?"

"Of course."

The answer was almost snapped at him, as if his question had been laden with implications.

"Everything will be all right."

"Dad, I long ago stopped worrying about Maurice. Everything always turns out all right for him."

"Things like this have a way of putting other things into perspective."

She looked at him warily.

"Amos has talked with Martha's mother."

"Martha's mother? I am Martha's mother!"

She screamed this, then turned and hurried away. George looked out from the waiting room.

"She's upset," Henry said.

"I heard her."

"I must learn to keep my mouth shut about Martha."

George did not comment on stupid remarks, or on most other kinds of remarks, for that matter.

Henry said, "I talked with Amos Cadbury."

"Ah."

George nodded and went off down the corridor after his wife. Incredibly, in less than an hour the operation was over, everything done with miniature remote devices, description of which made Henry feel that his own practice had not been far removed from the days of bloodletting. Well, of ether.

"It came off well?"

Wippel nodded. That five percent chance of failure seemed forgotten. Perhaps Sheila was right. Things usually did turn out all right for Maurice, eventually. Henry would have liked to tell Vivian of the young woman in California who seemed so close to their son, but now was not the time. Nor did he want to encourage the hope that Maurice would marry at last and father children who would be genuine Dolans.

The thought just came. Henry was thoroughly ashamed of himself. He actually beat his breast in contrition.

6

Amos Cadbury returned to his office to receive the good news of Maurice's successful operation. Henry chuckled over the phone when he said that Maurice would be out on the golf course in a matter of weeks. After he hung up, Amos turned his chair toward the window. The course of wisdom would be to go home and nap. He had slept fitfully on the flight back, but such sleep never truly refreshes.

He had done several things while in California, the first being to confirm that Maurice and Catherine Adams did share a condominium on the seventh fairway of the club of which Maurice was a member. She was not at the driving range when he stopped by, and he left a card and the number of his hotel. Finally, the woman's name and his conversation with Madeline Lorenzo had connected. When she called, he invited her to dinner. As they were led to their table, Amos was pleasantly aware of the eyes that followed them. Perhaps the other diners thought them a couple.

"Well," she said when they were seated. "What's the news?"

"Of Maurice?"

"Maurice, of course." She laughed at the jingle.

"The operation will take place tomorrow. I fly back in the morning. As soon as I have word, I will let you know."

"I should have gone back with him."

"Have you known him a long time?"

"Forever. I met him when I was an undergraduate at Northwestern. On a golf course, of course." She laughed again. "Everything I say rhymes."

"Did you know Madeline Lorenzo at Northwestern?"

The question did not visibly surprise her. She narrowed her eyes in thought. "There was a Professor Lorenzo."

"Madeline married him."

"How do you happen to know her?"

"She is a client of sorts."

She took a cigarette from a long packet and was about to light it from the candle on the table. She stopped, remembering California's draconian laws about smoking.

"We were roommates."

"Roommates."

She took an imagined carcinogenic drag on her unlit cigarette. "Lately, the past seems to be invading the present. I mentioned to you that Maurice and I had been in Chicago recently. Only a week and a half ago." She added this in a wondering tone. "A mutual friend of ours had died. A writer, Nathaniel Fleck. I was determined to be at his memorial." She smiled. "If only to annoy Maurice."

"Why would he be annoyed?"

She looked at him demurely. "He was jealous."

"So you and Maurice . . ."

"Live together."

Such a matter-of-fact statement would have been unimaginable when Amos was young, or even when he was middle-aged, and Catherine seemed almost surprised at his reaction.

"I've shocked you."

"A man my age has felt all the shocks that flesh is heir to."

"Shakespeare."

"Shakespeare. Do people who live together eventually marry?"

"It is my hope."

"Is that why you wanted to make him jealous?"

"I wonder if it will work." A terrible thought occurred to her. "Will he be an invalid?"

"There's not much danger of that, I'm told."

She sighed with relief. "I said that to ward off the possibility."

Now, in his Fox River office, Amos placed a call to the condominium on the seventh fairway and told Catherine Adams that all was well with Maurice. "I am told that he will be on the golf course again in weeks."

"I think I should go to him."

Amos said nothing.

"What do you think?"

"Why don't you wait a day or two? I will keep you informed."

He went home and showered and got into bed at four in the afternoon, where he lay sleepless, pondering the modern world. He remembered the newspaper account of the memorial for Nathaniel Fleck as well as what Madeline had told him of it. Only when he had decided to talk with Lieutenant Horvath about it was he able to fall asleep.

7

Tuttle parked his car in the driveway and sat looking at the impressive house, the manicured lawn, the molded shrubbery. A picture of affluence. He had been wise to decide to deal directly with Mrs. Dolan. But it was a man who answered the door. His look was not welcoming.

"Mr. Dolan?"

"Dr. Dolan."

"Of course. My name is Tuttle. Of Tuttle and Tuttle."

Dolan seemed to recognize his name, but not in a way that was reassuring.

"What do you want?"

"My business is rather confidential."

A woman appeared beside him. Tuttle swept off his hat, scattering calling cards. He picked them up and then addressed the woman. "Martin Sisk came to me, Mrs. Dolan. He employed me to find a certain woman."

"Martin Sisk!" Dr. Dolan angrily opened the door. "Come in."

Inside, Tuttle removed his tweed hat

again, carefully. The interior of the house was as impressive as the outside. Tuttle felt he was desecrating the white carpet when he walked on it. The Dolans led him into the living room, where Dolan took up a position before the fireplace.

"What is this about Martin Sisk?"

Tuttle felt it best to address the wife. "He came to me, on your behalf, Mrs. Dolan. Or so he said. I felt it wise to find out if that was indeed so."

"On my behalf?"

Tuttle shook his head. "Apparently my fears were not unfounded."

"What did he hire you to do?" Dolan demanded.

"That, of course, is a confidential matter."

"Then why are you here?"

"Was it about Martha?" Mrs. Dolan asked fearfully.

Dolan turned to his wife. "You had to talk about Martha with Martin Sisk."

She all but fell into a chair. "I had no idea . . ."

Dolan turned on Tuttle. "Now that you're here, you had better tell us what you have learned."

"You are asking me to act for you?"

"I have a lawyer. Amos Cadbury. Perhaps I should send you to him."

"Have you found Martha's mother?" Mrs. Dolan asked.

"I have."

Nothing was turning out as Tuttle had hoped. He should have refused to enter this house. The mention of Amos Cadbury had sent a chill through him. Thoughts of his last appearance before the local bar commission assailed him. A stern and forbidding Amos Cadbury had been on the committee that had considered disbarring Tuttle. He had escaped once more with only a severe warning. Another complaint could be his undoing. He sent up a prayer to his departed father.

"What do you intend doing with this information?"

Tuttle stood, assuming what dignity he could in the situation. "Dr. Dolan, I came here because, having been engaged by Martin Sisk to find the woman in question, I began to doubt the wisdom of simply telling him. These are delicate matters. As I told him, I have no wish to be party to anything that might tend to disturb the tranquility of people's lives." He addressed Mrs. Dolan. "Did you or did you not tell Martin Sisk to engage my services?"

The best defense is a good offense. He had found a way. Division between the Dolans was now his hope.

She tried to explain what had happened. Yes, she had talked with Martin, had confided in him. "But I didn't tell him to do anything! I didn't tell him to hire a lawyer."

"That puts me in a difficult position," Tuttle said, feeling the difficulty lift.

If they had been alone, Dolan might have taken his wife to task. The way he said Martin's name did not convey the idea that Martin was an old friend of the family who might have served as their intermediary.

"Tell us what you have found out," Dolan demanded.

"I will need to get a release from Martin Sisk in order to do that."

"Damn Martin Sisk!"

"Henry!"

"You should have known better than to confide in that sanctimonious idiot."

"Henry, we just talked."

"Talked!"

"Yes, talked. What's wrong with that, for heaven's sake?" She turned to Tuttle. "You have located Martha's mother?"

"Yes."

"Where is she? Who is she now?"

"As I explained . . ."

Henry Dolan exploded. "What is it you want, money?"

"I resent that, sir. I am a lawyer. The services of lawyers are engaged by clients. I assume that even doctors charge fees."

"How much?"

"You wish to become my client?"

"How much!"

"A modest retainer will do."

Dolan took out his wallet and plucked a fifty-dollar bill from it, and tossed the money onto the coffee table. Tuttle ignored it.

"Not enough?"

"Please, Doctor, that is unworthy of you."

Now Dolan slumped into a seat, glaring at Tuttle. His wife sat forward in her chair.

"Tell us where she can be found."

"Vivian, for God's sake, stop. Amos Cadbury knows who the woman is."

"Amos!"

"Of course. He has spoken with her. She is considering talking with Sheila."

"But Sheila will never agree."

Again the mention of Amos Cadbury chilled Tuttle. Even worse was the claim that the knowledge he had was already at the disposal of the Dolans, however unaware of it Mrs. Dolan had been. It helped that he was already on his feet.

"I think I should go. I came in good faith, but apparently that is not enough."

He strode across the white carpet toward

the front door, trying not to think of the fifty-dollar bill lying on the coffee table.

"Damn it, man. Stop. I will pay you for your troubles."

Tuttle had reached the front door. He had trouble opening it, but when he did, he turned to Dolan.

"I'll send you a bill."

Then he was outside and hurrying to his car. When he was in it, he wanted to lock the doors. Good God, what a fiasco. All his research had gone up in smoke. He started the car and backed down the driveway, a defeated man. But when he was in the street and shifting gears, he thought of his other client, Bernard Casey. His gloom lifted. His knowledge could still retain some power with young Casey.

8

On Saturday morning at breakfast, Marie chortled about the squabble between Martin Sisk and Grace Weaver the previous Thursday.

"Was it Thursday?"

"The Joyful Mysteries. That is how I remember."

"Do you ever say the Luminous Mysteries, Marie?"

"The what?"

"The new mysteries the pope has added to the rosary."

Marie's mouth became a firm line. Then she spoke deliberately. "The pope is a wonderful man and all that, but adding mysteries to the rosary is nonsense. The mysteries are what they are and always have been. Who needs new ones? It's part of the same nonsense that has almost ruined the Mass, change, change, change, as if people were bored."

"They're not mandatory."

Marie made a dismissive sound. As she pushed through into the kitchen, she muttered, "Luminous Mysteries!"

The young couple who had called were due at ten. Before they arrived, Marie, her insurrectionary thoughts forgotten, briefed Father Dowling.

"The Dolans, you've met. They were married here in the church. Before my time, of course. And the Lynches, too. Also before my time."

"So it isn't a matter of memory."

"I looked it up."

So had Father Dowling. He should have known Marie would anticipate him. "You would make a wonderful assistant pastor, Marie."

"Assistant pastor!"

"Pastor?"

But it was the recurring topic of women priests that vexed Marie, not the idea of taking a subsidiary role. Like many women, she was a harsh judge of her gender, and her reaction to the Luminous Mysteries was as nothing to what she thought of the agitation for women's ordination.

"Thank God the pope has stood firm."

"Luminously so."

She glared at him, and the doorbell rang, taking her down the hall to the front door.

Martha Lynch was a beautiful young woman, and Bernard Casey a handsome young man. Marie was beaming when she brought them to the study. Father Dowling rose and greeted them and pointed Martha to a chair.

Bernard remained standing, looking around the room. "I would say it is like a law library, but there the volumes all look alike."

"I have a degree in canon law. There are some legal volumes there, though not the kind you're familiar with."

"So you're a canon lawyer."

"For my sins."

"Do you know Amos Cadbury?"

"Amos is a dear friend."

"The only other lawyer I know in Fox River is a man named Tuttle."

"Tuttle!"

"You know him, too?"

"Only by reputation. It is difficult to think of him and Amos Cadbury as in the same profession."

Martha said, "We want to be married in St. Hilary's." She smiled radiantly as she said it. "It's a family tradition."

"So I understand. The Dolans are your grandparents?"

"They just love coming to the senior center. They have renewed acquaintance with so many old friends."

"Well, tell me about yourselves."

Each seemed as interested in what the other had to say as Father Dowling was. Their description of their families and their education gave a reassuring picture.

"How long does marriage preparation take, Father?"

"Well, it is up to the discretion of the pastor. Given your backgrounds, I think a few meetings will do. I would advise you to read the sections on marriage in the *Catechism of the Catholic Church.* I hope you have a copy."

"I kept mine from college," Martha said.

"Have you settled on a date for the wedding?"

They exchanged a look. Martha became solemn. "Father, I am only an adopted daughter of the Lynches."

"Only? That isn't an impediment."

"But I don't know anything about my real parents."

Father Dowling remembered his conversation with Henry Dolan in this very room. He had spoken to her father as well. A priest knows so many things from so many different sources, and the connections he makes must usually be confined to the privacy of his own mind. This lovely young woman's determination to find out who her birth mother was had particularly wounded

244

Mrs. Lynch but had brought anguish to the Dolans as well. Father Dowling smiled an enigmatic smile.

"I could say that none of us really does, but that isn't an answer you would accept. Why exactly does being adopted bother you?"

"It doesn't. My parents, the Lynches, have been wonderful to me. It's painful that they think I'm questioning that now. Mainly, I feel I owe it to Bernard."

"Then there's no problem," Bernard said.

"Of course you would say that. Father, Bernard's family accepts me because they know the Lynches and the Dolans. But what will they think when they find out I'm not really a Lynch, let alone a Dolan?"

"Have you asked them?"

Bernard said, "Martha, if it will make you feel better, I'll let them know."

"No. It must come from me. Of course, there are ways of putting these things that make it impossible for people to object. I know that. But I don't want that kind of waiver."

It was an unusual discussion between young people planning to marry, but Father Dowling found himself admiring Martha's disinclination to be thought something other than she was. The difficulty was determining the alternative.

"Surely you don't intend to remain single if you cannot discover who your mother was."

"I have to make an effort to find out."

"We are," Bernard said. He looked at Father Dowling. "I mentioned Tuttle. I've asked him to check local records and see if he can satisfy Martha's curiosity."

"You would have been better advised to ask Amos Cadbury."

"Oh, this is routine work, Father. It doesn't require a lawyer of Cadbury's stature. He would just pass it on to a junior in the firm anyway. This is something a paralegal could do."

"Thanks a lot," Martha put in.

He laughed. "A very good one, I mean." To Father Dowling he said, "Martha is a paralegal in our firm."

"Have you heard anything from Tuttle?"

"Not yet."

They went on to the business at hand. "You both understand that marriage is a sacrament, instituted by Our Lord himself . . ." They followed what he said intently, but it was clear none of this was new to them. Before the hour was up, Father Dowling felt that he could conscientiously have married them that afternoon. He told them as much.

"I'm game," Bernard said.

"Let's say that we meet several more times. Do the reading I suggested. There are some wonderful things by the Holy Father you will want to read as well. Meanwhile, decide on a date."

"Is your wedding schedule crowded?"

He smiled. "This is not the campus church at Notre Dame, Bernard. Here we have far more funerals than weddings. I am not suggesting an alternative."

Marie looked in and offered coffee, and coffee they had. Father Dowling got out his pipe.

Bernard said, "That explains the lovely lingering aroma in here."

"Oh, that would be Marie's cigars."

The housekeeper refused to be teased. Weddings had indeed become a rare treat at St. Hilary's, and Marie had clearly taken to this couple.

After they left, she said, "Blood will tell, Father Dowling. Blood will tell."

"Back to your kitchen, Dracula."

9

Amos Cadbury made the arrangements, and with some trepidation George Lynch went to meet the woman he had not seen since she gave birth to Martha. How those years seemed to have flown. George had a very different temperament from his wife's, but Martha's insistence that she must know who her real mother was had saddened him as well. Not that he didn't understand her desire. He found himself wondering about the young woman who had given them her child, and how the years had treated her.

Amos's account had been reassuring. "Her husband teaches philosophy at Northwestern. She has four sons."

"So you told me."

"Be prepared for an uncanny resemblance to Martha."

As he drove to Evanston from his laboratories, George told himself that he was on his way to report to Martha's mother on her daughter. He was proud of what Martha had become and was determined that Madeline Lorenzo should be proud as well.

Above all, he wanted her to see the wisdom of the difficult decision she had made so many years ago. It helped that she had all those sons.

It might have been Martha herself who turned to George when he entered the bookstore she had given as their meeting place. There were the same blue, almost green eyes, and the thick honey-colored hair. She even wore it in the same style Martha did.

"Mrs. Lorenzo?"

She looked at him quietly. What image of that fateful day had she carried with her? A woman in childbirth presents an elemental picture, but George had had a glimpse of her when Sheila went in to talk with her just days before the girl gave birth.

"Amos Cadbury told me how much like Martha you look."

She smiled. "Isn't it the other way around?" She took his hand. Holding hers, George, who was not an imaginative man, thought how unlikely a meeting this was. She led him to shelves along the wall. Literature. It was a used-book shop, one of the many in Evanston, as George had just discovered in looking for this one. She took a book from the shelf, as if to explain their being here.

"Your wife didn't come."

"She is taking this very hard."

"This?"

"Martha's wanting to know you."

"Martha. That's a lovely name."

"You would be very proud of her," George said. "She is a wonderful young person. I should have known that the time would come when she would want to seek you out. It isn't that she hasn't been happy, she has been, as we have always been delighted with her. Now that she plans to marry . . ."

"Marry!"

"Does that surprise you?"

"Come," she said. In the back of the store, coffee was available, and chairs in which to sit. No other customers were there. She took a rocking chair but sat forward, feet firmly forbidding the chair to rock. "I don't have to tell you how strange it is to be talking of her, Dr. Lynch."

"George."

"George. How often I have thought of her, wondered what she was like at this age and that. Tell me about her."

For George, Martha was an inexhaustible subject, and his reticence fled as he gave her the story of Martha's life. He might have been making an accounting of their stewardship. She followed what he said with great attention, her expression altering as he passed from peak to peak of Martha's accomplishments. George had the sense that he was reporting on Martha to an older version of herself. Finally, he came to Martha's employment at Foley, Farnum, and Casey.

"I'm surprised she didn't go to law school."

"She thought of that. She took the LSATs and was accepted at several law schools, Northwestern among them."

"We might have passed one another on the walk if she had. Why didn't she go?"

"She said it would seem she wanted a career."

"What does she want?"

"To marry." He looked at her. "To be what you are, I think."

"What a nice thing to say."

"You have other children?"

She nodded. "That is what makes this difficult. Of course, they know nothing of Martha." She paused. "My husband does."

"You mustn't think that Martha has any intention of disrupting your life."

"Oh, no. But then, disruption comes in many forms."

"I think if she could just talk to you, meet you."

"How I would love that."

"She could be taken for your sister."

Madeline smiled. "No. If we meet, there must be no more subterfuge."

"I think she would say the same."

"I would not tell her about her father. Never."

"She doesn't seem at all curious about him."

She looked at him with a half smile. "I am so glad we've met at last." Her brow clouded. "Her father is dead."

"Oh."

"Just recently. He was struck by a car in Fox River."

"Good Lord."

"He reappeared out of nowhere wanting to see our child."

After a moment she went on, telling him about their meeting. She shuddered at the memory. "He would have disrupted my life without a second thought. I went to Amos Cadbury to tell him Nathaniel had reappeared."

"Amos told me something of that."

"And arranged for us to meet."

"Yes. I hope this isn't too upsetting."

"I find it strangely consoling. As I said, my husband knows, but it isn't something we could talk about."

"Would you want to see Martha?"

"Want to? More than anything in the world. But I dread it, too. It wasn't easy for me to agree to see you."

"I suppose not."

"My sons," she said, and looked away.

That a woman like this should run the risk of becoming something less in her children's eyes seemed to George the height of injustice. He wanted to tell her not to agree, but that would be to betray Martha. His natural taciturnity saved him the need to say anything.

"I have to think about it. My husband doesn't know of our meeting, but I couldn't see Martha unless he agreed." She rocked once in her chair, then rose. "Thank you so much for coming. I know this must be difficult for you as well."

"I wanted you to know about Martha."

"Thank you. Now I want to see her all the more."

They parted outside, where she said she would let Amos Cadbury know what the next step, if any, would be.

10

Bernard Casey's reaction when Tuttle telephoned the young lawyer made Tuttle wish he had taken this course at first. His disastrous visit to the Dolans had not done much for his self-esteem. Their mention of Amos Cadbury brought the fear that they would tell the dean of the Fox River bar about his going to them. No doubt Dolan would portray it as an effort to shake them down. As the event receded into the past, Tuttle's estimate of his own performance lessened. He had got in a few good licks, but what was the point? His exit line was a bluff, of course. Any attempt to extract payment from Dolan would doubtless bring Cadbury into the fray. Wistful thoughts of that fifty-dollar bill, tossed disdainfully on the coffee table, were difficult to expunge from memory.

"How much should I bill Martin Sisk for?" Hazel asked when he told her he had reported to his client.

"Use a heavy hand." He blamed Martin for his embarrassment with the Dolans.

"Well, you said he was loaded. So you found the woman he was looking for?"

Tuttle had not put Hazel wholly in the picture of late, not something easily done. How could she criticize him if she didn't know what he was doing? But there had been some truth in what Tuttle had said to Martin and then to the Dolans. He did not wish to be the instrument of disturbing innocent lives. Tuttle's childhood had been a happy one, in memory even happier than it had truly been. His mother had been forty when she bore him, and he was accordingly cherished the more — their little Isaac, as his father had called him. Much as he loved his father, Tuttle seldom revealed his Christian name. It didn't sound Christian at all. Besides, the allusion was all wrong. When Tuttle read the account in Genesis of Abraham taking *his* son Isaac to Mount Moriah to offer him in sacrifice, he thought of how unlikely it was that his father should have acted on such a dream. His father's unwavering support while Tuttle fought his way through law school had increased his son's sense of family ties. With his father, he had often visited his mother's grave and found nothing odd in the way his father had talked aloud to her as if she were there with them. Perhaps she was. But it was his father's presence that Tuttle often felt now, his counsel he invoked, his name that explained the TUTTLE & TUTTLE on his door. Tuttle had come away from the Dolans ashamed, feeling his father's disapproval of what he had done.

Bernard Casey was another matter. His interest was merely to satisfy the curiosity of the woman he intended to marry. Surely there was no threat in that to anyone.

"Same place?" Casey asked when Tuttle called.

"Water Tower Place."

"At the top of the escalator."

Casey was waiting for Tuttle when he rose from street level. They went again to Starbucks, where Tuttle took care in sipping his coffee. Once burned, twice shy. He might have been thinking of his visit to the Dolans as well.

"So you've located her?"

"I have."

Casey waited. Tuttle turned his paper mug on the table before him, looking for true north. He lifted his eyes to Casey.

"Is something wrong?" Casey asked.

"No. I have learned the family is not anxious for the young lady to have this information."

"Martha isn't likely to cause anyone trouble, you know."

Tuttle had not met Martha Lynch. The thought that by telling her he might avenge himself on the Dolans he rejected out of hand. "I have also learned that the family knows the identity of the woman. Amos Cadbury has spoken with her."

"And they refuse to tell Martha?"

Tuttle shrugged. It was seldom that conscience made him cowardly, but now he felt a strange reluctance to reap the fruits of his research. "I had to make a trip to South Bend."

"For the adoption papers?"

"You knew they had been registered there?"

"The Lynches showed that document to Martha, but it doesn't identify her mother."

"That document was in Fox River."

Casey shook his head. "Amos Cadbury is a very cagey lawyer."

"The best," Tuttle said despite himself.

"Look, Tuttle. You're my lawyer, I'm your client. This is between us. Of course you will be compensated for your work. I'm impressed."

The young man's attitude removed all barriers. Tuttle said, "Her name is Madeline Lorenzo now. She lives in Evanston."

"Married?"

"With a family. Her husband teaches at the university."

"Ah. I can appreciate your caution." He had made notes on what Tuttle told him in a little leather notebook with bronze corners and a yellow ribbon. He looked up. "I would prefer that you didn't send the bill to me at the firm. This is my home address." He jotted it on the back of a business card and gave it to Tuttle as he rose to leave. "Good work, Tuttle."

Tuttle remained with his cooling coffee. Why didn't he feel a sense of triumph? Casey's praise had warmed his heart, and he did not doubt the young man's discretion. But there were so many currents running in this situation, someone was bound to be hurt.

11

Mark Lorenzo's philosophical interests had taken him a long way from those large questions that first interested him, as an undergraduate, in the world's oldest discipline. What does it all mean? Where have I come from, where am I going? Is death the end? His youthful mind had risen to the challenge of such questions, but graduate work and his subsequent research had led him into narrower alleys. Madeline had likened his interests to crossword puzzles. Perhaps she was right. Little in the real world was altered by recounting the pros and cons of the behavior of adverbs in ethical discourse. No matter. For most people, the answers to the large questions were provided by religion, always a greater consolation than philosophy.

Marriage to Madeline had brought him back to the faith of his fathers, and recent events had made ignoring the great unsettling questions impossible. It was in this very office that Madeline's supposed friend, Catherine Adams, had come to him long ago.

"Perhaps Madeline has mentioned me?"

"You are roommates."

"I had you for epistemology."

"And you want your money back?"

"Oh, no. It opened my mind."

"An open mind is an equivocal blessing."

She sat back and tipped her head to one side. "So you do talk that way even when you're off duty."

She was flattering him, of course. Flirting, too, in a way. The feminine arts were often innocently used to affect a grade, but she was no longer his student.

"How did you do in epistemology? I don't remember."

"You gave me an A."

"I don't give A's. You must have earned it."

"De omnibus dubitandum est."

"I hope you don't believe that."

"Just practicing my Latin."

"You've studied Latin?"

"On Madeline's behalf."

"I don't understand."

"She took a semester off, so I took the class for her."

He thought about it. "I suppose that is possible."

"Oh, I took two courses for her. She did well in both."

"Leave of absence."

Her eyes widened. "I supposed she had told you."

"No."

"She went to student health, but she refused to take their advice. And mine."

He waited, trying to remain casual.

"Of course, she's Catholic," Catherine went on.

"So am I."

"Then you will understand why she had the baby."

What a venomous little actress the girl was. Mark was now determined not to afford her the satisfaction of bringing such news to him. "To understand all is to forgive all."

"Then she told you."

He became a character in Trollope. "My dear young woman, Madeline and I have no secrets from one another. We are going to marry." Thus might Abelard have spoken of Heloise. Mark felt as unmanned as the fiery medieval logician by what Catherine Adams had told him, but he was damned if he would let her know it. "Now then, why have you come?"

She hardly missed a beat. "I have an epistemological problem."

She chattered on, dredging up puzzles

261

from his lectures, and he played the game. Somehow the visit ended.

"I can't tell you how relieved I am," she said with a significant look when she stood at his door.

"The benefits of epistemology."

What man could receive such knowledge of the woman he was about to marry and be unaffected by it? Still, the manner in which he had learned helped ease the blow. There seemed little doubt that Catherine Adams had brought him this story with something other than a benevolent end in view. Well, her time bomb had not detonated. He said nothing to Madeline. How could he mention it if she had not? And so they married, and in the chapel was Catherine Adams, all smiles and gush.

He and Madeline had kept her secret, separately, over the years. Their own children erased that past. Mark came almost to believe that Catherine's tale had been a lie, but a conversation in the faculty lounge with Foster, the classicist, proved otherwise. Had he ever had Madeline in class?

"Tall willowy girl with long hair?"

"Is that a translation?" It was a good description of Catherine.

He had never pursued the matter further. He was ashamed of having put the question to Foster. The essence of marriage is trust. He did not need Madeline certified. Fortunately, Foster was lured away by North Carolina, so the danger passed that he might meet Madeline, remember Mark's question, and wonder what had happened to the tall willowy girl with long hair.

Time's arrow flies in only one direction, but memory is a different story. The past never really goes away if it can be recalled. Now the past had returned bodily, first Nathaniel and then Catherine putting in an appearance, having a seismic effect on Madeline. The one bonus of this unwanted revival of the past was that now Madeline knew that her secret had been his all along. He had received a credit he did not feel he deserved, but he had never felt closer to her than when she then sobbed with relief in his arms.

The thought of Catherine's visit and then of Madeline sent him home. He would have lunch with her. He found her sitting in the living room. The drapes were pulled, and the gas log in the fireplace was lit. Apparently she hadn't heard him come in, and for a moment he stood looking at his wife, beautiful in the flickering light from the fireplace. He called her name, and she continued to stare at the fire.

He tried again.

"Madeline."

She held out her hand without turning. He took it and knelt beside her chair. "What is it?"

"When I turned on the gas I waited a bit before lighting it. What a whoosh it made." She spoke in a dreamy voice.

"You have to be careful of that."

"I thought of not lighting it." She turned to him. "Isn't that awful?"

"Let's have some lunch."

She didn't move. "A lawyer called."

"A lawyer."

"Bernard Casey. He wanted to come see me. About Martha."

"For the love of God, when will this end? Madeline, you have to see that girl. We can't go on like this."

"The boys."

"Don't underestimate the boys. Besides, it isn't obvious that any announcement has to be made. Either way, all this hush-hush has got to stop. Martha is not going to forget about it. She is as determined as you would be."

Madeline nodded. "That's what I think."

"What exactly did the lawyer say? Who is he acting for?"

"He's her fiancé, Mark. They're going to get married."

"What did he want, your blessing?"

"He wants me to talk to Martha."

"Then do it, for God's sake. Tell him to set it up."

"I did."

"When?"

"She'll call me." She looked at him. "Imagine hearing her voice on the phone."

"Let's drive out to Rockford and have lunch at the Clock Tower."

"The car is still in the garage."

"We can borrow Stephen's four-wheeler."

"That's getting to be a habit."

"Well, we paid for it."

"I'd rather fix you lunch."

"Just a thought."

12

Cy had not forgotten the hit-and-run on Dirksen when Phil Keegan told him Amos Cadbury had called and asked if he could stop by and talk about it. "I don't know what his interest is, Cy. I didn't ask. He might have started to quiz me about it, and you handled it. There's nothing new, is there?"

"No."

"I figured you'd tell me if there was. He wanted to come here, but what the hell. Go talk with him."

"When does he expect me?"

Phil gave him a slip with a telephone number. "Just call and tell him when you can stop by."

There was nothing new on the hit-and-run, but Cy reviewed what was old before calling Amos Cadbury. The paint the lab had scraped from the parking meter that the vehicle had grazed when it bounced down off the curb after striking Fleck was in a plastic bag in the evidence room.

"You want me to keep that?" Zeller asked.

Zeller was in charge of the evidence room. Most of his day was spent leaning out of the dutch door of his domain, watching other people work. He had a year to go until retirement and had finally landed the assignment he had always wanted.

"You in the habit of throwing evidence away?"

"Only when bribed." Zeller bared his crooked teeth in a smile. He was one rung up from Peanuts Pianone in Cy's book. He dropped the plastic bag in a tray but didn't take it away. "I been thinking, Cy. Why the hell should I retire now that I've got this?"

"It would give you a chance to rest."

"We always thought Florida, but now Madge needs a new hip." Madge had been a meter maid when Zeller married her. Was that a choice, Florida or a new hip?

Cy went down the hall to the cafeteria and saw, as he had hoped he would, Pippen at a table with a book opened in front of her. Her habits were well known to him, thanks to steady if unobtrusive observation. Even so, he pretended to himself that it was just by chance that he ran into her. Pippen was as married as he was, and would have been astounded to learn that she represented a remote occasion of sin for him. Cy bought a bottle of mineral water and joined her. She looked up, smiled, and closed her book.

"Madge Zeller is going to get a new hip," he told her.

"I hope they can find the old one."

Cy smiled. Madge was a bit of a hippo. "Remember the hit-and-run on Dirksen a couple weeks ago?"

Pippen tapped the book. "This is one of his novels. Nathaniel Fleck. You'd think he would have used a pen name."

"Is it that bad?"

"His name, not the book. It's pretty good. A little steamy, but they all are now."

Cy turned the book toward himself and opened it. *The Long Good-bye.* "That sounds familiar."

"He stole the title. He says so in the fore-word."

Cy turned a page. There was a dedication. *To Catherine. Ave atque vale.* "What's that mean?"

"Hello and good-bye? Something like that."

"What's it about?"

"I'm only half done. The woman loves a guy, has for years, and now she has a rival, someone from long ago, before they met. He has this dream that that old girlfriend had his baby and he ditched her and now . . ."

Well, you get the picture."

"You ought to write reviews."

"We're going to discuss this in my reading group."

"Your reading group."

"Doctors' wives have to pass the time somehow."

"But you're a doctor."

"They made me an honorary member. When the author was killed here in town, someone suggested we ought to read his latest."

"I'll wait for the movie."

"What are you detecting lately?"

"A body was found in the trunk of a car parked near the old depot."

"Why wasn't I told?"

"Lubins handled it. This was last week. You and whatchamacallit were whooping it up in Mexico."

"You ought to take the missus there, Cy. It was wonderful."

"I'll think about it."

"My husband's name is Madison."

"The Ojibwa."

She laughed. "Ob-gyn. Well, at least you remember his specialty."

Before he called Cadbury, Cy dialed the St. Hilary's rectory and asked Father Dowling what *ave atque vale* meant.

"Hail and farewell. It's from Catullus's poem to his dead brother. Don't tell me you're reading Catullus, Cy."

"Who was he?"

"A Roman poet."

"Are those words Italian?"

A pause on the line. "Latin."

"Thanks."

"Niente."

"More Latin?"

"Italian."

Amos Cadbury wanted to hear about the memorial for Nathaniel Fleck held at Northwestern. "I understand you were there, Cy."

"They gave him quite a send-off."

"Lots of speakers?"

"Lots and lots."

"Did you hear the woman, Catherine Adams?"

"She was the honorary widow."

"Tell me about it."

Cy told Cadbury what he could remember. Mainly he remembered the effect she had on the audience. "They seemed to like the fact that she had never married the guy."

"She say why not?"

"Who needs a slip of paper when you're in love? Something like that."

"She came all the way from California for the occasion."

"I suppose."

That was about it. After he left, he had the impression that Amos Cadbury had been trying to suggest something. But what?

13

Maurice Dolan had been moved to a private room, where he held court as he recovered. Vivian spent much of the day at her son's side, and there was a steady stream of visitors.

Martha came by with her young man. "This is my worthless uncle, Bernard."

"Watch it. I'm precious. I'm willing my body to science. They can't believe how well I came through the operation. You golf, Bernard?"

"More or less."

"Come on, you must have a handicap."

"Twelve."

"That's more less than more. We'll have to play a round before I go back to California."

Martha was astounded. "How soon do you expect to play again?"

"Soon. Within weeks."

"What's your handicap?" Bernard asked him.

"I'll have to give you a few strokes."

Martha made an unflattering noise. "Bernard, he's a scratch golfer."

"Only when I itch."

Martha and Bernard were still there when Catherine Adams appeared. She stood in the doorway, staring at Maurice, as if waiting for him to notice her. When he did, she flew across the room and took him in her arms. Vivian followed her in and watched this scene with maternal approval. She joined Catherine Adams at bedside, and Maurice made the introductions.

"Henry has told me all about you," Vivian said.

"Mrs. Dolan, what a shock this must have been."

Vivian continued her appraisal of this beautiful woman. Maurice said, "And that is my niece, Martha."

Catherine turned, and when she faced Martha her eyes widened. "Your niece."

"My sister Sheila's daughter," Maurice said.

Catherine took Martha's hands and held them. "I feel I already know you. Isn't that odd?"

"And this is Bernard Casey. My fiancé."

"Oh, what a ring!" Catherine was still holding Martha's hands.

Vivian looked on beaming, as if her dream of one big happy family were finally coming true.

"Maurice, tell us about Catherine," Martha cried.

"Don't you dare."

"Oh, Catherine and I go way back. Way, way back. And now we're in business together." Maurice told Martha and Bernard about the golfing range in Huntington Beach, a real gold mine, a gusher, the smartest move he'd ever made. "Thanks to Dad, of course."

"I love your hair," Martha said to Catherine. "Of course, you have the head for it. I wouldn't dare have mine cut so short."

"I should hope not. Don't ever let her cut it, Bernard. It is exactly as it should be."

"Do you golf, too?" Bernard asked.

"Not like Tiger there, but yes, I golf. Maurice would go out every day of the week if he could."

Vivian said, "Now I am determined to visit California myself."

And so it went on. George looked in, fresh from the OR, and blinked at the gathering.

"And I thought you might be lonely."

He was introduced to Catherine. "You're a doctor," she said.

"Pathology."

She looked at Maurice. "I thought you said anesthesiology."

"That's my father."

"Well, I won't need his services. I'm still groggy from the flight."

"You must stay with us," Vivian urged. "We have plenty of room. And we can talk."

"I'd love it. Maurice?"

"Be their guest."

"I left my bag downstairs with the receptionist. I came directly from the airport."

"That is so thoughtful," Vivian said. "I'll get you settled. You can always see Maurice."

"That's the plan."

Bernard had to go back to the Loop, but Martha stayed, and in twenty minutes she was alone with her uncle.

"Would you rather I leave, too?" she asked.

"Stay. The only thing worse than watching daytime television seated is watching it lying down. Bernard's nice."

"Isn't he? But what about Catherine?"

"What do you mean?"

"She seems to be making a claim."

"We're close."

"As pages in a book?"

"Hey."

"Well, you always were a rogue. Are you going to marry her?"

"Maybe I will, now that I'm losing you."

"You're a nut."

"Any developments?"

She leaned over and whispered in his ear. "I'm going to meet her."

"Good."

"Now that it's arranged, I'm frightened."

"How do you think she feels?"

14

Martha told Father Dowling that she now knew who her mother was and was going to meet her.

"At last."

"And now I'm nervous. Just wanting to know has caused so much commotion, I wonder what meeting her might do."

An imaginary real mother might well be preferable to the woman in the flesh. Still, Father Dowling admired Martha Lynch for her persistence.

"Do your parents know?"

"The Lynches? Just my father. He's already met her."

"So you won't be entirely surprised."

"His main point was that we look very much alike."

In fact, the taciturn George Lynch had come to the noon Mass the day before and into the sacristy afterward. He declined an invitation to join the pastor for lunch — "I have to get back to the lab" — so they talked in the sacristy.

"Martha says you have already met

Madeline Lorenzo," Father Downing said.

"You know her name."

"A priest is told so many things."

"My fear is that Martha will next want to know who her father was."

"That might be more difficult," Father Dowling said carefully.

George Lynch then turned to his ostensible reason for coming into the sacristy. "She tells me that she wants to be married here, Father. I'm glad. Sheila and I were married in this church, and her parents before us. As the father of the bride I want you to know that I will take care of everything, all expenses. I want it to be a memorable wedding. Like my own."

Father Dowling assured him that his expenses would not come from the parish but from florists, caterers, dressmakers, perhaps chauffeur-driven cars.

"Henry and Vivian speak so warmly of the way the school is now being used. Do you ever hold receptions there?"

"There's no reason why not. You will want to speak to Edna Hospers and secure the date."

George went off immediately to speak to Edna about it, and Father Dowling went to his lunch.

"I thought you were lost," Marie greeted him.

"Between the porch and the altar?"

Marie had long since learned not to respond to allusions she did not catch. Father Dowling ate his solitary lunch and afterward prepared to go out. Marie's eyebrows rose in a question. It was tempting not to tell her where he was going, but that would have been unwise. It was important that she know where to reach him. Edna might worry that the old people in the center could suffer an injury that would involve the parish insurance, but Father Dowling sensed that for the elderly one of the perhaps unconscious attractions of coming here each day was the proximity of a priest. At their age, the awful summons might come at any time, and they would want to leave this world fortified by the sacraments of the Church.

"I'll be at St. Joseph's Medical Center, Marie."

"What's wrong with calling it a hospital?"

"I'll ask."

Marie shook her head. Circumlocution was another sign of the times. As he drove across town, Father Dowling thought of the German word *Krankenhaus.* No ambiguity about that.

Henry Dolan had spoken to Father Dowling about Maurice. "I'm afraid he might have drifted away, Father. Until recently, he has been a great disappointment to us. And to himself, I think. Perhaps this operation is a blessing in disguise."

Like many a concerned parent, Henry wanted a priest to bring his child back into the fold. Not an ignoble desire, certainly, but a commission usually difficult to fulfill. For all that, Father Dowling was anxious to meet the young man of whom he had heard so much — not all of it flattering, except when Martha had spoken of her uncle.

"Moving to California was the wisest thing he ever did," Martha said. "If he had done it long ago, everything would be better. Families can be very oppressive. Not on purpose, maybe, but my grandparents never let up on Maurice."

"He is settled down in California?"

"And there is a woman who seems to have designs on him."

"Ah."

"I kidded him that we could have a double wedding."

Martha gave him a little sketch of Catherine Adams that concentrated on her haircut. "She's just flaky enough to be right for him." Martha spoke of her uncle as if he were a difficult boy, probably something she had learned at home.

Before going upstairs, Father Dowling looked into the chaplain's office. Lance Higgins, in corduroy trousers, a coat sweater, and sandals but wearing a Roman collar, greeted him warmly.

"How's the *Krankenhaus?*"

Higgins laughed. He was in his thirties, one of the younger priests who were the hope of the future, always a joy to visit. "The house of cranks? Truer than you'd think. Do you have a parishioner here?"

"I came to see Maurice Lynch."

Higgins's smile grew broader. "What a guy. He seems to have spent his life on the golf course."

"Maybe he has a vocation."

Talking with Higgins could be corrupting. He laughed at every joke, particularly the bad ones.

Higgins closed the door. "He just shook his head when I asked if he'd like me to bring him communion. You know how rare that is nowadays. Of course, I would have found out first if he was in shape." Higgins was indeed of the new breed that so vexed Andy Greeley and the aging crowd of clerical rebels. "His mother seems concerned about him."

"Was it a serious operation?"

"Wippel talks of it as routine, but if anything had gone wrong . . . Well, it didn't. Maurice Lynch came through it beautifully."

There was a young woman with a crew cut sitting with Maurice Lynch. She rose from her chair at the sight of Father Dowling, showing the slight uneasiness a priest is used to.

Father Dowling went to the bed and told Maurice who he was. "Martha has told me all about you," he added.

"Lies, lies. You will marry her?"

"That's right."

The locution startled the young woman. Maurice laughingly explained and then introduced her. "Catherine Adams."

"Ah, your fiancée."

"My what?"

Catherine Adams lifted her brows and smiled prettily at Maurice. "You might have told me."

"It was Martha, wasn't it, Father? What a matchmaker."

"I like Martha," Catherine said emphatically.

"Maybe it was Amos Cadbury."

"Honestly," she said. "In this town everybody knows everybody else." She launched into the story of Amos and Henry Dolan coming to California to fetch Maurice.

Amos had been such an old sweetie, she said. "Maybe I'll marry him."

"I thought I was the older man in your life."

"No, the handicapped one."

"Every golfer is handicapped. Catherine has made a career deceiving two men into thinking she's nuts about them. Well, now my rival is gone."

"Maurice!"

He assumed a serious look. "Sorry. A bit of a tragedy, Father. And right here in River City. Our friend was run down on the street."

"Not Nathaniel Fleck?"

Catherine cried, "Don't tell me you knew him, too!"

"Only the name."

"And such a name. He wouldn't listen to me when I told him he should use a pen name. Reginald Hedge or something like that."

"It doesn't seem to have prevented his success."

"I'm sorry I brought him up," Maurice said.

"And you ought to be."

There was an easy intimacy between the two, but it seemed to take place a level or two above real seriousness.

When he said good-bye, Father Dowling entered into the banter. "I'll be in my rectory if you need me."

Catherine was standing beside the bed. She took Maurice's hand. "What's wrong with here?"

"Maurice will explain."

On that ambiguous note, he went off down the hall. Maurice seemed arrested at the prep school level, but Catherine Adams was more difficult to read. Obviously she had not welcomed talk of Maurice's dead rival, if that was what Nathaniel Fleck had been. Ah, the modern world.

15

If every event were recorded, the world would soon be swamped by the accumulation. Of course, computers reduced everything to tininess, so the past did not submerge the present. In any case, it made police work easier. Cy Horvath was being assisted by a chubby young woman — Charlene, according to her name tag — who sat at the computer in the airline office in the Loop.

She said, "Give me that date again."

Cy began with the day before the memorial. Charlene clicked keys, and the monitor became a blur of activity, then steadied.

"From LAX?"

"Los Angeles, yes."

"There were four flights into O'Hare from there that day. Adams?"

"Catherine Adams."

She leaned toward the monitor as she slowly scrolled. She shook her head once, then twice. Finally, four times. She looked up at Cy. "Zilch."

"Why don't we just go back to the day before, and then the day before that, and —"

She was already doing it. Her fingers flew; flights and passenger lists appeared; she scanned them and shook her head. She struck oil when she had gone back five days before the memorial at Northwestern.

"Could you print that out for me?"

"Let me see your ID again."

Cy opened and shut his wallet.

"That was fast."

He opened it again. She looked from the photograph to him. "I hope the picture on your driver's license is better."

She punched a button, and the printer began to whir. When it stopped, she tore a page free and handed it to him.

"Thanks."

"Aren't you going to tell me?"

"No."

She shrugged.

He said, "It's just routine." He folded the printout and put it in his jacket pocket. Then a thought occurred to him. "Do you have a record of rental cars?"

"Of course not."

He thanked her again and left. In his car, he sat behind the wheel and got out the passenger list Charlene had given him. Adams, Catherine. All it proved was that she hadn't walked or driven from California. She had arrived in midafternoon. Where had she stayed and how had she gotten there? O'Hare was ringed with hotels, and courtesy vehicles took passengers back and forth to them. The thought of checking them all — and, if he drew a blank, all those in the Loop — was not inviting. Maybe she had stayed in Evanston. That wasn't much help. To put off the evil day, he decided he would try the rental car agencies. They all had offices in the Loop, so that simplified it somewhat.

He got out of his car and went back inside. Charlene looked up in surprise.

"Let me use your phone book. The yellow pages."

"You look familiar."

"You've seen my photograph."

She pulled the directory out of a desk drawer and plunked it on the counter. "Adams is spelled with an *A*."

"So is Avis."

He found the appropriate page and began to jot down numbers. "Could I use your phone?"

"This is getting to be like a citizen's arrest."

"That isn't what it means."

"Dial nine for an outside line."

He dialed nine several times, identifying himself and asking each agency if they had rental records there. The answer was always the same. "It's all on the computer."

At the agency that tries harder, the second he went to, a girl who reminded him of his protégé Agnes Lamb did what Charlene had done at the airline, with the difference that he knew what date he wanted checked. The girl peered at the monitor and shook her head. "Nope."

"Sure?"

"Yup."

"Thanks."

That was the answer he had got at his first stop. He got the same answer at the other agencies. So he was back to the daunting number of hotels. The thought of Agnes suggested that he go back to Fox River and let someone else do the donkey work.

Agnes Lamb just looked at him when he told her what he wanted.

"You want all these hotels called?" He had helpfully opened the yellow pages for her. There were pages of hotel listings. "Even Peanuts could do this."

"I doubt it."

"So do I. Can I have help with this?"

Cy rounded up three secretaries, including Phil Keegan's. He thought of putting

Zeller on it, too, but rejected the idea. He left the four surly women and went to see if Dr. Pippen was busy.

"You're back to the hit-and-run?" Pippen asked.

"It's a slow day."

"What about the body in the trunk?"

"It'll keep."

"Ha ha."

She went over her report for him in great detail, and he followed carefully, hoping some inspiration would come. It didn't.

"What did you expect, a tire tread on the body?"

All he had was that plastic bag with paint removed from the parking meter the vehicle had grazed after putting Fleck through the window of the coffee shop. But that was useless without a vehicle to match it with.

Agnes Lamb looked in, all smiles. "The Hyatt Regency in the Loop."

"How long did she stay?"

Agnes glanced at her notes. "Looks like a week."

"Not even Peanuts could have done better."

Agnes stuck out her tongue and left.

"Isn't she beautiful?" Pippen said.

"All girls are beautiful."

"I'm a girl."

"No, you're not. You're the assistant coroner."

"Don't rub it in."

"It's better than being an Ojibwa."

"Who was staying at the Hyatt Regency?"

"Another beautiful girl."

That night, he watched television with his wife. After they went to bed, when he was almost asleep, inspiration came. Well, a hunch. He got out of bed, took the printout from his jacket pocket, and went into the bathroom with it. Catherine Adams topped the list. He let his eye run down it and found what he hadn't known he was looking for. Lynch, Maurice. If the list had reflected seating assignments, the names would have been side by side.

"Cy," his wife called drowsily. "Is anything the matter?"

He went back to the bed, got in, and patted her thigh. Then he lay wondering what the significance of his discovery was. The elation he had felt in the bathroom drained away. It probably didn't mean a thing.

16

"Five hundred," Tuttle said when Hazel asked him what to bill Bernard Casey.

"You're crazy."

"Three hundred?"

"A thousand! You can come down if he complains."

"Then charge Martin Sisk the same amount."

"With pleasure."

"Not during office hours."

"That creep hasn't called me for days."

"Any more irate girlfriends?"

She ignored him. The hope that Martin would take Hazel off his hands was fading. Maybe he could bargain.

"Make out the bill for Sisk, and I'll deliver it in person."

"I could do that."

A tempting alternative, but Tuttle rejected it. Indirection seemed more promising than unleashing Hazel on Martin. She made out the bill, put it in an envelope, and handed it to him. "Tell him it's a letter bomb from me."

"Patience, Hazel, I told you, you've made a conquest."

"We'll see."

Tuttle drove to St. Hilary's and parked by the former school. What had once been the playground was filled with the elderly, moving slowly from one basketball net to the other. Tuttle pushed through the door and into a large room where a variety of games were being played. There was the click of billiard balls and the slap of cards, a rattling from the shuffleboard game. It seemed an argument against growing old. Martin was leaning over the billiard table, lining up a shot. The reaction to Tuttle's entrance communicated itself to him. He looked up; his cue moved involuntarily, and he missed his shot. His opponent chortled, then noticed Tuttle, too. Good God, it was Henry Dolan.

The doctor strode toward him.

"What do you want now?" he asked with controlled anger.

Suddenly Dolan's wife was at his side. Tuttle felt like cast off gum they had stepped in. Tuttle looked past them to Martin and beckoned to him. Martin shook his head frantically. A little silver-haired woman came and took his cue, and he darted away from her and headed for the door. Tuttle followed. Martin scampered across the parking lot. Tuttle caught him as he was trying to unlock the door of his car.

Martin wheeled on him. "Are you crazy, coming here?"

The Dolans, too, had come outside, with the little silver-haired woman. Tuttle went around Martin's car and pulled open the passenger door. Martin was behind the wheel.

"We better get out of here, Martin."

This advice was taken. They drove past the three witnesses at the door, and Tuttle tipped his hat. He was retrieving calling cards when Martin bumped out of the parking lot and drove up the street out of sight, then stopped.

"What the hell is this, Tuttle?"

"I bring a message from Hazel."

"I don't want any message from Hazel!"

"I can hardly tell her that. After what's happened."

"What do you mean?"

"Gentlemen never tell, Martin. But ladies do."

"It's a lie."

"Gallantry will get you nowhere."

"The Dolans told me you had been to their house. What I had to endure! But everything was back to normal, and now you show up."

"Who is the little lady with the silver hair?"

"She is none of your business."

"I ask, of course, on behalf of Hazel."

Martin turned. "Tuttle, you have to call her off. Please." There was desperation in Martin's popping eyes.

"She sent you this."

Martin looked at the envelope with dread. "I won't accept it."

"Better read it before you decide."

Martin tore open the envelope and extracted its contents. He looked at Tuttle. "This is a bill." He looked at it again and then became earnest. "If I pay this, will you call her off?"

"That seems reasonable."

"I'll send you a check."

Tuttle smiled and shook his head. "Hazel would never forgive me if I returned empty-handed."

"Damn it!" But he brought out his checkbook and opened it. "Do you have a pen?"

Tuttle handed him a ballpoint. Martin balanced the book on the steering wheel and wrote as swiftly as this permitted. He signed his name with savage finality, then tore out the check.

"Here."

Tuttle accepted it in his doffed tweed hat, which he then returned to his head.

"My car is in the parking lot by the school."

"I can't go back there."

"Do you think it will be easier later?"

Martin made a U-turn and headed back to the senior center, creeping in at 20 mph. But the trio was no longer outside the entrance. When Martin had parked, Tuttle hopped out.

"Thanks for the lift, Martin."

"Go to hell."

Tuttle went whistling to his own car. He sat in it for a moment, watching Martin approach the entrance warily.

When he was inside, Tuttle got out his cell phone and put through a call to Peanuts. "What do you say to the Great Wall?"

"Now?"

"Ten minutes."

The phone went dead. Tuttle put his car in gear and set off. Describing the recent scene to Peanuts would be as nothing to telling Hazel.

When he and Peanuts were settled in a booth at the Great Wall, he got out his phone again and called his office.

"Martin wants you to call him at the senior center at St. Hilary's. Just have him paged."

He signed off.

The humiliation of his visit to the Dolans seemed at last behind him. Of course, he had blamed that fiasco on Martin Sisk.

17

Henry Dolan was so furious that the lawyer Tuttle had shown up at the senior center at St. Hilary's, he swore to George that he'd never go back. "That fool Martin Sisk went off with him. To think he had hired such a charlatan. He came to the house and tried to hold me up."

George had heard the story from Vivian. He was always the recipient of news that concerned Martha, Sheila's reaction being what it was. She had gone into the bedroom and slammed the door when George told her again she must meet with Madeline Lorenzo. At least she hadn't locked it.

He went in and sat on the bed. "Putting your head in the sand won't change anything."

"I don't want to talk about it."

"It's beyond talk, Sheila. You should talk to her before Martha does."

"Martha." She lifted her head from the pillow into which she had been crying.

"A meeting has been arranged."

She sprang from the bed. "That ungrateful child!"

You're only thinking of yourself. He didn't say this aloud, of course. His mission in life was to pacify Sheila, as it had been to devote himself to Martha. Sometimes he half feared that there was something unwholesome in his love for the child he had brought from the delivery room and put in Sheila's arms, making them parents of a sort, mother and father. Pathology is an impersonal specialty, a matter of running tests on biopsies in the course of an operation or performing autopsies. He had chosen the residency in pathology over several others just because it would protect him from dealing with living patients. That had left him free to devote himself exclusively to Sheila and Martha. Of course, Sheila was devoted to Martha, too, but he had come to see that his was a more selfless love than hers. Martha's curiosity had from the beginning seemed a threat to Sheila, whereas George had always been sympathetic. Of course she would want to know the woman who bore her. If Sheila thought that belated meeting could destroy the long years they had had with Martha, then she was very much mistaken. Increasingly, it became clear that it was of herself she was thinking, not Martha.

George recognized this without condemning his wife. He expected that others would be weak while he was strong. He could hardly have felt as deeply as Sheila the news that she would never herself carry a baby to term, but he had felt it. During her unsuccessful pregnancies, he had scarcely dared dream of the joys of fatherhood that lay ahead, so moved was he by the prospect. Acquiring Martha had been their salvation. How could Sheila imagine they could lose her love now?

"What is she like?" Sheila asked.

"Martha."

"Oh, stop saying that!"

It was as if no father had been involved in the making of Martha, so like Madeline was she. He had never told Sheila who the father was. At the Women's Care Center they had spoken to George more as a doctor than as the prospective father, telling him that Madeline's pregnancy was the result of an affair with a fellow student. "Of course, he refuses to take responsibility." Irene made a face. "Men!" In the circumstances, her misogyny seemed justified. Irene had gone on: The father was a big man on campus, despite his ridiculous name.

"Ridiculous?"

"Fleck." She spat the name. Perhaps that

was why he never forgot and why he had been startled to see the name on a book Sheila was reading.

"What's this?" he'd asked.

"Just a novel."

George had learned not only the name but to hate it as well. It was all he could do not to rid his house of a book by the author who was Martha's father. Sheila had wanted to expunge memories of the Women's Care Center from her mind, the better to forget how Martha had come to them. George's gratitude led him to continue to volunteer to counsel young women there once a week, a secret he kept from Sheila. He felt that he was paying both their debts to the place. Irene had passed away, rest her soul, but the work went on. George had been at the center when Nathaniel Fleck came, making inquiries.

"What did he want to know?" George asked Louise, who had succeeded Irene.

"Nothing I could tell him."

"Something about a child?"

"What else?"

"Did he know the mother's name?"

"Doctor, I wouldn't even listen to him. As you know, everything here has to be kept completely confidential. We owe it to the young women."

George had informed himself of Nathaniel Fleck's career since coming on that novel of his. The Internet is a marvelous device. He entered Fleck's name in Google and pressed SEARCH, and almost instantaneously he had his choice of sites devoted to the author. Eventually, he checked them all. They were repetitious, of course, but uniformly laudatory. When Fleck showed up at the center, George felt he already knew him.

He caught up with Fleck in the parking lot. "I'm Dr. Lynch, a counselor here."

"I just got the bum's rush."

"Can I help you?"

"I'm sure that woman could have helped me, but she wouldn't."

"Try me."

They went to a bar and drank beer, and Nathaniel Fleck bared his soul, such as it was. George became sure that the man had a romantic dream he wished to realize, an experience he wished to savor; that others might be affected by its realization seemed not to have occurred to him. He seemed to think he could rewind the years and undo what he had done, but it was only of himself he thought. It grated on him to know that he had been such a coward. He even quoted from Gatsby after his third beer. "Can't repeat the past? Why, of course you can."

It became clearer and clearer that the man was a menace, not only to Martha but to Madeline as well.

18

Cy wouldn't have dared to ask Agnes and the other women to repeat the process he had gone through with car rental agencies, so he did it himself. Luckily, in all but one case he found a different person on duty from the day before. The girl at Avis was the same.

"Not you again?"

"It's habit forming."

She was a lot of woman with a small, pretty face. Lisa. She looked speculatively at Cy. Unobtrusively he splayed his left hand on the counter. His wedding ring made her businesslike.

"What was the name again?"

"Maurice Dolan."

"Bingo."

The car had been rented the same day Maurice and Catherine arrived from Los Angeles. It had been turned in the day Catherine went home. The payment had been made with her credit card.

"Just so they pay," Lisa said.

He used her phone to call the Hyatt Regency and got someone unwilling to give out the information he requested, certainly not on the telephone, so Cy went down there. The place was a zoo, two buildings divided by a street, with an underground passageway between them. It took him a while to find the office.

"I talked to Mr. McDonald on the phone."

"Mr. McDonald is not available just now."

Cy showed Miss Quirk his ID.

"Where's Fox River?"

"Do you want me to get a court order?"

"Oh, for heaven's sake."

She seemed pleased when there was no record of Maurice Dolan having stayed in the hotel on the dates Cy gave her.

Cy went through the passageway and sat in the lobby, an echoing atrium with music coming from somewhere. A lousy place to think. Perhaps the couple had shared the room Catherine Adams had taken in her name. Perhaps. The adverb of futility. He had begun the day in pursuit of Maurice Dolan, and all he had was a rental car and a room in her name. Only the airline record put Dolan in the area at the crucial time.

Maurice Dolan had just returned from physical therapy when Cy came into his room. "Can I ask you some questions?"

"Who are you?"

He showed Dolan his ID. Maurice took it and studied it, which was his right. "Questions?"

"I'm investigating a hit-and-run that took place two weeks ago."

Maurice Dolan went to the bed and hoisted himself onto it. "So what are the questions?"

"What kind of car did you rent from Avis?"

"Why should I tell you that?"

"Why shouldn't you?"

"Because you're investigating a hit-and-run."

"What do you know about it?"

Maurice shook his head. "You're fishing."

"And you're dodging."

"I think I'll call the family lawyer. Amos Cadbury."

"He's a good man. I'll be back."

At the Avis garage, he asked the attendant about the vehicle rented in Catherine Adams's name.

"You want to rent it?"

"What condition was it in when it was turned in?"

"That information would be in the office."

"Let's look."

"Geez." But he led the way through the parked cars to the glassed-in office and consulted the records. He looked at Cy. "Nothing here. They didn't fill the gas tank before turning it in."

"Where is that vehicle now?"

Once more the computer made the question answerable. "It's out."

"Who's renting it?"

Cy got the name and the local number of the renter. His name was Winston Heather, and he wasn't cooperative. "You want it back? Forget it, I'm not done with it."

"I just want to see the vehicle."

"You want to see the vehicle."

"That's right."

"Well, you're going to have to come here, because I sure as hell am not going to drive it to the airport so you can take a look at it."

He was staying at a Holiday Inn near the Indiana line in an area of casinos. Cy located the vehicle in the parking lot. He looked around and then got out his penknife and scraped some paint off the fender, near a spot where the underlying metal showed through because of a dent. Back in his car, he called Heather and told him he had changed his mind. He hung up on the profane response.

19

Martha's mother was a moody character, but Bernard Casey liked her father. They had golfed together twice, and Bernard liked a man who didn't chatter on the golf course. He doubted that George Lynch chattered anywhere.

When they came off the ninth green, George just looked at him, and Bernard shook his head. "Let's go right on to ten."

No doubt George would have been equally amenable if he had suggested they pop into the clubhouse for refreshments. When they got to the tee, George bent over the water fountain for a long time. He had the honors, being one of those golfers who took the shots he could and made the most of them. He put his ball 150 yards out in the fairway. He would be on the green in three and doubtless get his par 5. Bernard's drive was powerful and long, and inaccurate. They got into the cart and drove to George's ball. Bernard watched his future father-in-law take out a 6-iron and advance his ball to the green. Another shot like that and he would be next to the pin. They went in search of Bernard's ball.

"Have you ever golfed with Maurice?" Bernard asked.

George nodded.

"I like him."

"Everyone likes Maurice."

"Too bad he's going back to California."

"It's best."

"Is he serious about that woman, Catherine Adams?"

George had no opinion on the subject. The only topic that elicited much talk from him was Martha. George had asked Bernard what he thought of having the reception at St. Hilary's.

"It can be on the moon, so far as I'm concerned."

"St. Hilary's isn't the moon."

"George, I think it's a great idea."

"We all went to school there." He meant Sheila and himself, and his grandparents, too. A family tradition.

Bernard wondered what George really thought of Martha's obsession with finding her birth mother.

"Of course she should know her. They look like sisters, you know."

Bernard had to waste a shot getting his ball onto the fairway. His third shot landed on the green but rolled beyond. George hit a 7-iron, and his ball ended twelve feet from the hall.

"Good shot."

"You swing like Maurice."

"I thought he was pretty good."

"He is very good."

Still, the comment seemed a criticism. George meant he was trying too hard, and he was.

"What does she think of all this? The mother?"

"This can't harm her. I would be as concerned to protect her as I am to protect Martha. The woman was treated very badly by a thoughtless young man."

This was a speech from George. Bernard thought that any woman George was determined to protect would be protected indeed.

In the clubhouse afterward they had a sandwich and iced tea on the veranda. From the course, the sweet smell of grass came to them.

George said, "Tell me about your work."

This was pleasant, Bernard thought, reporting to his future father-in-law. It seemed only right after the paces his family had put Martha through. Bernard had yet to tell his parents that Martha was adopted, not the natural child of the Lynches, and he was annoyed that he had not. The Martha he had fallen in love with was here and now, herself, not a bundle of inherited genes. Bernard was proud of his family but young enough to regard himself as a self-made man despite the advantages he'd had. Surely he would have been taken on by the firm right out of Notre Dame law school even if his father hadn't been one of the titular partners.

George listened to his account with genial interest. "I never thought of anything but medicine myself."

"What does a pathologist do, exactly?"

"You wouldn't want to know."

"That bad?"

"Not entirely. It was the lab work that drew me." Now George had all the pathology work in Fox River and in the abutting suburbs; employing nearly a hundred people, his clinic was housed in a new building strategically located for access from those suburbs. "Not that I do much myself anymore."

Just so, Bernard's father sometimes lamented the fact that he no longer did the donkey work the younger lawyers in the firm did. Casey senior was a star of the Chicago courts, putting to effective use the work of those youthful lawyers as he argued his case.

"Someone I would very much like to meet is Amos Cadbury."

"He will be at your wedding."

"He is a hero to my father. The fact that Cadbury had attended the Notre Dame law school is the reason I went there, urged by Dad."

They sat in silence then, a comfortable silence. Bernard's future looked as serene to him as the fairway he looked out upon, its surface mottled by sun, altering with the passage of clouds.

"Martha sees her tomorrow."

"Good."

20

Hearing her mother's voice on the phone filled Martha with the strangest feeling. She had dreamed of this, and of what was coming, and now she was almost frightened. She said as much.

"I feel frightened, too. You mustn't expect too much," Madeline said.

"Where shall we meet?"

"I could come to you."

Of course, Martha could not go to the Lorenzo home. Martha was at last aware of how her curiosity affected other people, but she detected nothing of resentment in Madeline's voice. She thought of the parish grounds at St. Hilary's, the walkways and benches scattered about, the shrine to Mary, a shaded, pleasant place.

"Do you know St. Hilary's parish?" Martha asked.

"In Fox River?"

"That's where the wedding will be." Silence on the line. Should she send Madeline an invitation? She could not yet know if the invitation would be welcome.

"We could meet there."

"In church?"

"No, no. There are benches and shady places. It's very peaceful."

"All right."

Martha went to the noon Mass, having taken the day off from Foley, Farnum, and Casey. The night before, she had confessed to Bernard her fright.

"Think of how she must feel," he said.

"Of course." How wonderfully Bernard had taken all this. At the moment, she could have called the whole thing off. She had spoken to her mother on the telephone, two strangers bound by the ties of blood. Almost, that seemed enough. If Bernard had shown the least disapproval, she *would* have called it off.

When she came out of the church, Martha wandered toward the grotto, the place of assignation. There was still an hour before her mother would come. She sat on a bench and took out her lunch. Someone sat beside her. She turned and knew immediately that this was her mother. They stared at one another in silence for a minute, and then Madeline held out her hand. Martha took it, still studying this face she had so longed to see, this woman who had brought her into the world. Neither of them spoke for several minutes.

"You brought a lunch," Madeline said.

"Because I meant to be early."

"I saw you at Mass."

Then they were in one another's arms, and Martha was flooded with joy. Embracing Sheila could never be like this. This was her true mother. She could not see for the tears in her eyes. When she sat back she saw that Madeline was crying, too.

A flood of words came from both of them. Madeline talked of that difficult time so long ago when so many had urged her to solve her problem with an abortion. Her eyes rounded in horror at the thought. "They said I was stupid to have you."

"Do you think you were?"

This was fishing for compliments, but Martha was shameless. Once more she was in her mother's arms.

Some distance away on the walk a figure stood. Father Dowling. Impetuously, Martha beckoned him to them. He hesitated but then came up to the bench on which they were seated.

"Father, this is my mother!"

Father Dowling bowed. "So you have met one another at last?"

"Now everything is perfect."

"You sound like God in Genesis."

Madeline laughed. What a lovely laugh it was. Martha could scarcely contain her joy. Whatever image she had formed of her mother, the reality was ever so much better. And everything had happened so easily. She explained that both of them had come earlier than agreed.

Madeline said, "Now we sound like the third little pig."

"Father Dowling is preparing us for marriage. Oh, you must come to the wedding. You have to meet Bernard."

"I think I should leave you," Father Dowling said. He waved — it might have been a blessing — and then went off to the rectory.

They shared Martha's lunch. Madeline told her about Mark and the boys.

"I have brothers!"

"Martha, you must understand that they do not know about you."

"It doesn't matter. This is all that matters." She leaned toward Madeline and kissed her cheek. "Tell me everything."

The life that Madeline described seemed one that had been meant to include her, but of course that was nonsense. Martha thought of that other man, her father, but she did not dare mention him. Who had told her that she and Madeline might be sisters, twins? George. Was it true? Oh, she hoped so.

"But I want to hear about you," Madeline said.

"There's really nothing to tell."

"I'll be the judge of that." A little wry smile.

To Martha, her own life seemed uneventful, but Madeline nodded her along as she spoke of school, of college, of Foley, Farnum, and Casey, and of meeting Bernard.

"I did catch glimpses of you from time to time, Martha."

"You did!"

"I couldn't resist it when I found out who the Lynches were and where they lived. No names came up when . . ."

"You saw me," Martha said in awe. The desire that had driven her had not been absent from Madeline after all. It was clear that she had been very brave to have her baby, and even braver to give it up, but it was something she could never put out of her mind.

"And of course I wouldn't have caused any trouble to your parents. You have been very fortunate, Martha."

After Father Dowling left, others had gone past on the walk from time to time.

Now someone had stopped. Martha turned from her mother.

"Martha!"

It was Sheila, a prissy little man at her side. Her remark had been prompted originally by surprise at seeing her daughter here. Then she took in Madeline and a look of agony spread over her face. Her eyes darted from one woman to the other.

"This is my mother," Martha said.

"Your mother! I am your mother. You ungrateful girl." She actually shook her finger at Madeline. "I will never forgive you for this. After all we have done."

"Mother," Martha cried, and both women looked at her.

"Mother?" Sheila said. "Am I your mother?"

"Oh, for heaven's sake, can't you see how wonderful this is? Do you remember Madeline?"

Sheila's angry glance seemed to leap across the years. The little man with her had followed the conversation as if it were a tennis match.

Now Madeline held out her hand to Sheila. "Mrs. Lynch, I have no wish to cause you pain."

"Pain?" Martha cried. "She should be delighted."

Sheila slapped her. Her hand moved as if she had no control over it, and when she saw what she had done she stepped back, horror-struck. Then she turned and hurried off down the path toward the school. The little man skipped after her. Martha and Madeline were silenced by what happened.

After a moment, Madeline said, "I understand her reaction. Does she think I have come to take you away?"

"Oh, I wish you would."

"No you don't, sweetheart. That can never be. You must make it up to her. It won't be long before you go off with Bernard."

PART FOUR

1

Father Dowling heard of the arrest of Maurice Dolan from Phil Keegan. "Cy never gives up, Father. What a detective he is."

"He thinks Maurice Dolan ran over that author?"

"It's not just thinking anymore. Dolan has confessed."

"Good Lord." Father Dowling thought of the man he had visited in his hospital room and found this news difficult to accept.

"The man has been in and out of trouble all his life," Phil said with the air of a man with long experience of the effects of original sin. "Nothing like this, of course, but great oaks from little acorns grow."

"I don't think that is the meaning of the phrase, Phil. Why on earth would he have done it?"

"Jealousy."

Phil's initial report was so casual that Father Dowling permitted himself to think his old friend might be mistaken, not that he didn't share Phil's admiration for Cy

Horvath's tenacity. It was Amos Cadbury who provided the details that made the story plausible.

"What makes it delicate, Father, is its connection with recent events you and I have discussed. I can tell you that Nathaniel Fleck was the father of the child we know as Martha Lynch. Madeline and Catherine Adams were roommates at Northwestern when Madeline got into trouble. At the time, Catherine was seeing much of Maurice Dolan. Apparently, Fleck then won the young woman's heart. The animosity must have begun then, and yet the three of them remained friends of a sort. When Maurice and Catherine also moved to California, they renewed regular acquaintance with Fleck, and that is when the trouble must have begun."

"A rivalry?"

Amos nodded. A young man in Amos's firm, James Kilkenny, was representing Maurice, but the accused and then confessed killer of Nathaniel Fleck had, against Kilkenny's advice, unburdened himself to Cy, once the accusation had been made. Catherine's lifelong infatuation with Fleck, episodic until recent years, had increased in California. She was determined to marry the author, so Maurice was out in the cold.

"But didn't they come to Chicago together?"

"Then Fleck was killed. That seems to have brought them together again. No doubt as Maurice Dolan had hoped."

"He actually confessed that he ran the man down?"

"Oh, his confession will play no role in the trial. The plea will be not guilty. Kilkenny intends to concentrate on the ambiguity of the accident that killed Fleck."

"Accident."

"I know, Father, but you must think in legal terms. Kilkenny wants to make the best case he can. A vehicle out of control, an unintended death. To be found guilty of involuntary manslaughter is preferable to cold-blooded murder."

Amos's heart was not in this explanation, though. That the law permitted and even demanded fine-grained distinctions was one thing, but to fabricate a story to make a guilty man innocent was something else entirely.

"Has Maurice Dolan agreed to all this?"

"Not yet, I gather, but Kilkenny will doubtless make him see the wisdom of it."

"I would like to speak to Maurice."

Amos nodded his approval. Father Dowling could offer consolations unavailable to the law.

An abject Henry Dolan begged Father Dowling to see his son. Henry seemed to have aged ten years under this new burden. His daughter's flare-up when she had come upon Martha and Madeline Lorenzo on a bench near the parish grotto had been the talk of the senior center ever since. Sheila had gone there to find her parents, still hoping to prevent Martha from seeing her birth mother, and Martin Sisk had offered to take her to the church, where the Dolans must have lingered following the noon Mass. On the way, they had come upon the joyful reunion, made into a fiasco by Sheila's hysterical reaction.

"I have spent my life trying to get that boy out of trouble," Henry said. "There seems no way out of this."

2

Catherine Adams was staying with the Dolans and getting along just fine with Vivian.

"This used to be Maurice's room," Vivian said as her guest was settling in.

Catherine looked around. "Where are the golf trophies?"

"Oh, he took such things with him."

The first morning they sat long over the breakfast table while Henry read the *Sun-Times* in the living room. Vivian was intent on finding out just how matters stood between Catherine and her son. She liked the self-possession of the young lady and how easily she fitted in. In age, she must be close to Maurice, but wasn't that better than his settling down with some chit of a girl?

"So you and Maurice are partners?"

"I'm just a silent partner, Vivian."

"And what do you do when you aren't silent?"

"I'm a financial counselor."

Henry perked up at this and came back

into the dining room. Catherine smiled at him as he sat. She gave a brisk little description of her work.

"I hope you're managing Maurice's money," Vivian purred.

"He says he doesn't have any."

The Dolans laughed in chorus. Henry said, "Most of it is just in prospect, of course. What he now has is in a trust arranged by Amos Cadbury."

"Well, the sly old thing."

"Maurice's has been a checkered career," Henry said.

"Oh, I know all about that."

Vivian said, "And how long have you two known one another?"

"Forever. I was an undergraduate at Northwestern when we first met."

"That long ago?"

Catherine laughed. "Don't ask how many years it has been."

They laughed together, all three.

Catherine said to Henry, "When you came to California to take Maurice back here, Amos Cadbury stayed on."

"One look at the plane I brought Maurice home in and Amos said no thanks."

"Such a wonderful man."

The Dolans took turns telling her how wonderful Amos Cadbury indeed was.

"He seemed intent on finding out about me and Maurice."

"And what did he find out?" Henry asked.

"He didn't report to you?"

"Report to me? Please don't think I put him up to it."

"Things have been simplified of late."

"Oh?"

Catherine leaned toward Vivian. "You would think that the longer you knew a man, the easier it would be. It's not. And my problem was that there were two."

"Two!" Vivian exclaimed.

"Someone else I had known since Northwestern."

"Nathaniel Fleck?" Henry said.

Catherine feigned surprise, but only for a moment. "But of course you would know all about what happened to poor Nathaniel."

"Who is poor Nathaniel?" Vivian wanted to know.

"Sheila lent you one of his books, Vivian."

"He's an author."

"Was," Catherine said, and sipped her coffee with her eyes downcast.

Henry went into the living room and returned with a copy of *The Long Good-bye*. Vivian looked at the book. "Oh, I hated that story. I couldn't finish it."

Henry had opened the book. "He dedicated it to you," he said to Catherine.

"Yes."

"The book just came out."

"Books are written at least a year before they come out."

"Ave atque vale."

Catherine nodded. "We had finally agreed to part."

Vivian was trying to make sense of this. "Had you been engaged to this other man?"

"Engaged? Oh, nothing so formal. No more than I am to Maurice."

Having brought things to this point, Vivian was determined to go on. "No more than?"

Catherine put her hand on Vivian's and smiled. "You will be the first to know. As I said, things are different now."

"With Fleck gone?"

"Exactly."

Vivian had to settle for this, but she was content. Henry was now used to the close-cropped hair on the shapely head of the young woman.

"I have met George Lynch but not your daughter."

Vivian looked grave. "Sheila has been going through a very difficult time."

"Oh?"

Henry took his paper back to the living room. Vivian's whispered account was audible where he read, but he made no effort to follow what she was saying.

Catherine repeated Madeline's name when Vivian said it.

"Yes."

"A lovely name."

"And she is a lovely woman. As is Martha."

"Martha I met. At the hospital. And her young man."

"That is what precipitated it all, her coming marriage. She just had to know who her mother was."

"No wonder Sheila is upset."

This was in the morning. In the afternoon, they heard that the police had visited Maurice. By the time Henry and Catherine got to the hospital, he had confessed to striking Nathaniel Fleck with a car on a downtown street.

3

Cy Horvath had been surprised when Maurice Dolan reacted as he did to the questions put him. He had listened silently, following closely what the detective said.

"You rented a car?"

"I think you already know that. I suppose you located it?"

"We did. It had been rented to Catherine Adams."

Maurice had sat up slowly and swung his legs off his bed while Cy talked. Now he looked out the window for a time, then smiled.

"That little tent of blue which prisoners call the sky. Do you know the phrase?"

"No."

"It's from 'The Ballad of Reading Gaol.' "

"I'll take your word for it. Who drove the rental car, you or Catherine Adams?"

"We both did. Not at the same time, of course." His smile had become almost wistful. "All right, Lieutenant, you got me."

"Got you?"

"I did it."

"Did what?"

"I ran down Nate Fleck with that car."

"It's not a joking matter," Cy said.

"Indeed it's not. I'm perfectly serious."

"Tell me about it."

He closed his eyes for a moment and then began. He had been parked on Dirksen, waiting, and when Nathaniel Fleck came along the walk, he moved after him. "When I saw my chance, I jumped the curb, struck him and then sped away."

"He went through the window of a coffee shop."

"I read all about it."

The newspaper accounts could have provided all the details of Maurice Dolan's story, and Cy found himself skeptical. Maurice Dolan's confession came too easily, and for all his melancholy manner as he spoke, he did not seem sorry for what he claimed to have done.

"I suppose you had a motive."

"Oh, yes. The usual thing. Jealousy."

"What were you jealous of?"

After hearing it himself, Cy got on the phone and called Jacuzzi, the prosecutor. Jacuzzi brought a stenographer, and Maurice went through it all again, for the record.

Maurice had taken Catherine out while she was an undergraduate at Northwestern and he was an ABBA. Asked to explain the acronym, he said it meant that he had acquired college credits but no degree. All but BA. The affair had gone on peacefully until Catherine was attracted by a fellow student, Nathaniel Fleck. Thus began what Maurice called a "scrimmage à trois" that lasted for years. For a time, Catherine was his, but Fleck then would steal her away. Two years ago, the contest seemed over. Catherine, weary of her way of life, was determined to settle down and marry Fleck. The difficulty was that Fleck, having triumphed, found victory less than he had expected. His ardor cooled. It was not helped when he lost a good deal of money following Catherine's advice. Then a rival emerged against whom Catherine had no chance. "It's all in his last book, the one he dedicated to Catherine, giving her the final kiss-off."

Jacuzzi said he would rather hear it from Maurice than read the book.

"I'm glad Nate isn't here to hear you say that."

In *The Long Good-bye*, Fleck had told the story of a man who, years after the event, is plagued by memories of a girl he got in trouble. As he broods about it the conviction grows that somewhere in this world there is a child he fathered, a child who would now be twenty and more. He is determined to find the child. His mistress tries mockery to dissuade him, pleads with him, threatens him. To no avail. He tells her it is all over. If it takes the rest of his life, he intends to find his child. "That was the reason for Fleck's trip back here."

"So it wasn't just a fictional story?"

"What is fiction but the truth disguised. I'm quoting Nate."

"And Catherine followed him."

"And I came along. Her big hope was that Nate would be unsuccessful and things could go back to where they were."

"Leaving you out in the cold?"

Maurice pointed at Jacuzzi and nodded. "Bingo."

"Did Fleck find his child?"

"Only its mother. And she would tell him nothing. Of course, that only strengthened his determination."

"Who is the mother?"

At this point, Maurice Dolan's volubility stopped. "What difference does it make?"

"You don't know?"

Maurice looked at Jacuzzi. "Nate didn't confide in me. Why should he?"

The stenographer read his statement back to Maurice. He listened with great interest, making minor corrections and additions, and that was that.

Jacuzzi took Cy into the hallway. "Book the son of a bitch."

"Can you use his confession?"

"In court? Of course not, but he gave you a road map for your investigation. You did tell him he could call a lawyer?"

"I told him."

Maurice was on the phone to Amos Cadbury when they went back into the room. An officer was posted outside.

Someone had alerted Tetzel, and the reporter for the *Fox River Tribune* got in to see Maurice. Thus it was that Maurice's confession was splashed all over the pages of the afternoon newspaper.

4

Maurice's confession earned a small mention on the local television news, and credit was given to the *Fox River Tribune* for the story. Mark Lorenzo found a copy of the paper and brought it home, and he and Madeline read it with their heads together. Their three younger sons were occupied elsewhere in the house, two doing homework in their rooms, Joel, the youngest, watching baseball in the rec room in the basement. Stephen, of course, was in his campus residence.

"He kept us out of it," Mark said, and Madeline squeezed his hand.

"So far."

She looked at him. No need to say it. Catherine Adams would hardly be so discreet when the police talked to her. The bomb that had been slowly ticking for several weeks was about to go off.

"What can we do, Mark?"

"I'm going to talk to that detective who came to my office, Horvath."

"What good will that do?"

"He's a good man."

"Maybe if we do nothing . . ."

"It will be better if I talk to him."

"We'll have to tell the boys."

He thought about it. "Maybe."

He called the Fox River police and left a message for Cy Horvath. They were at the dinner table when he called back. Mark went into the kitchen to talk with him.

"You've solved your crime," Mark said.

"We have a confession."

"I wonder if we could get together."

"Did you read the account in the local paper?"

"Yes."

"That's all he said."

"He's her uncle, isn't he?"

"He was asked who the woman was Fleck came back to see and just clammed up."

"Has Catherine Adams said anything?"

Horvath got his point. Mark asked again if they could talk. They arranged to meet at a sports bar across from the courthouse in Fox River in an hour.

"You work nights?" Mark asked.

"I'll be there."

Mark was more than ever convinced that Horvath was a good man. He called Stephen and asked to use his car.

"The Neon's still in the garage?" Stephen asked.

"I haven't picked it up yet."

"You ought to get a real car, Dad."

"Why, when I can use yours?"

Luck was with him, and he found a parking space right in front of the bar. No need to pay the meter at this time of day. Horvath stood at the bar with a pint of Guinness before him, watching the ball game. He acknowledged Mark's arrival, then asked, "What'll you have?"

"That looks good."

When his Guinness had settled, they took their glasses to a booth. Horvath looked receptive.

"You can understand my concern, Lieutenant."

"I understand."

"If Catherine Adams is interviewed, she's likely to mention my wife. I told you what she's like."

"What do you want me to do?"

Mark looked at the creamy foam on his Guinness. "I don't know."

"Maybe you should talk with her." That made more sense than coming to Horvath, but Mark was glad to have a chance to talk with the detective.

Horvath described the way Maurice

Dolan had told his story. "He ought to write fiction himself," Cy said.

"Don't you believe him?"

"What is fiction but disguised truth?"

Mark stared, and what served as a grin came over Horvath's usually impassive face. He explained the origin of the remark.

"I don't know where I can find Catherine Adams."

"She's staying with the Dolans." He explained who the Dolans were. "You want to go over there, I'll come along."

They finished their beer and went outside. Horvath said he would drive them to the Dolans.

"Let me just be sure my car is locked," Mark said.

Horvath looked at the SUV. "I thought you drove a Neon."

"This is my son's."

"They ought to be outlawed."

Horvath expanded on his opinion of SUVs on the way. "Anyone driving a sedan with one of those behind him gets the full benefit of the headlights right in his rearview mirror because of the height of the vehicle." Horvath spoke with conviction if not passion. They arrived at the Dolans's, and he swung into the driveway.

The man who came to the door was

338

Henry Dolan. Cy Horvath began to identify himself, but the doctor waved him in. "I know you."

Dolan seemed to think Mark was another detective, and Horvath did not explain. All he said was "This is Lorenzo."

Vivian Dolan was a basket case. She looked at Horvath with hatred when she understood who he was.

"Catherine Adams is staying here, isn't she?" Horvath asked.

"She went off to the hospital as soon as we heard. Amos Cadbury says Maurice's confession is useless."

"He means it can't be used in court."

"You can't convict a man just because he says he's guilty."

"That's right."

Henry Dolan seemed relieved at Horvath's ready assent. Momentarily. "Is there something else?"

"Physical evidence."

"My God."

"You say Catherine Adams is at the hospital?"

Vivian suddenly spoke. "She intends to be at his side no matter what!"

Outside again, Horvath said. "You want to come with me to the hospital?"

"Yes."

The officer stationed in the hall intercepted Horvath. "They've been trying to find you."

"Yeah?"

"Go on in. You'll see why."

Maurice Dolan, in a robe, sat stiffly in a chair. Catherine Adams was on the edge of the bed. She turned when they entered, Cy first.

"I'm Horvath."

"Finally! Did you take down this idiot's so-called confession?"

"You mean Maurice Dolan?"

"Don't listen to her, Lieutenant. She's overcome with nobility."

"Oh, shut up." She stood and faced Horvath. "I rented that car. It was in my name."

"I know that."

"Well, know something else. It wasn't Maurice who ran down Nathaniel Fleck. I did. And by God I'm glad I did."

5

The hitherto unsolved hit-and-run on Dirksen Boulevard had now been solved, unfortunately because two people had confessed to it. Phil Keegan was not amused.

"You'd think the two of them planned it this way. One confession meant to neutralize the other."

"Can't it be resolved?"

"There is some physical evidence, but that would only confirm the identity of the vehicle."

"Would?"

"The lab sent it downstate when they weren't happy with the results. But as I say, it won't matter much. They both claim to have driven the vehicle."

The present hope was to locate one or the other somewhere else when the hit-and-run had happened. Cy Horvath was working on that. Meanwhile, Father Dowling went down to St. Joseph Medical Center, stopping first to talk to Father Higgins.

"As soon as I heard, I went up and urged him to make his peace with God," Higgins said.

"And?"

"He said not yet."

Make me chaste, Lord, but not yet? According to Maurice's confession, he had killed Nathaniel Fleck to rid himself of a rival in his pursuit of Catherine Adams, but by confessing he had ensured a long separation from her if he were convicted. Well, perhaps not too long, if Kilkenny's machinations were successful.

"Did you talk to Catherine Adams?"

"She's not Catholic."

Father Dowling went up and was let into the room by the police officer on duty. Maurice Dolan was alone.

"Ah, Father Dowling, come in."

"Father Higgins says he has spoken with you."

"I'm afraid I shocked him."

"That's unlikely." It never seemed to occur to laypeople that priests were privy to every breach of the Decalogue. Often, the most hair-raising stories were whispered through the confessional grille. They were almost a relief from the routine peccadilloes of the frequent confessors. "So you have confessed?"

"Not to Father Higgins."

"Don't you think that would have been a good idea?"

"It's been too long to enter into it lightly."

"Waiting can be risky when you have a weight on your soul. Of course, now you have competition in the matter."

He threw up his hands. "Dear Catherine. She would do anything for me."

"Even confess to murder?"

"The charge won't be that severe, I'm told."

"By Kilkenny?"

"Amos Cadbury's myrmidon."

"The police fear that the two of you, you and Catherine Adams, are playing a game."

"I suppose it can seem that we are."

"Are you?"

"Catherine is, at any rate. Nate Fleck had been the fly in the ointment too long. A recurrent rival. Pretending to cut her off forever was inspired, and she rose to the bait. I decided to do something about him."

"Then Catherine has a motivation equally strong, if not stronger."

"A woman spurned? She always did live in a fantasy world. We had quite an argument when she came to visit me. Even then I didn't dream she would do what she has done. Unfortunately, that detective, Horvath, showed up and she told her story."

"So Fleck's latest novel is the key to it all."

Maurice Dolan became suddenly serious. "Father, I don't know if you realize the commotion that has been going on in my family."

"Because of Martha?"

"Yes. She has to be kept out of this! I have to warn Catherine not to bring her into it. If she does, if she causes even more anguish than there now is . . ." He paused. "You'd have to know Martha to understand how I feel."

"But I do know her. She plans to be married at St. Hilary's."

"Ah, that's right. I met the young man. Very midwestern, but nice. I wonder if Sheila understands enough to be worried. Something a lot worse than she feared would result from Catherine's telling the whole story. That is why the police mustn't take her seriously."

Was Maurice Dolan's motive to be found here, if his confession were false — the protection of his niece, Martha?

"Is Catherine Adams still staying with your parents?"

"Isn't that ironic?"

"In what way?"

"They may have taken an adder into their nest."

Father Dowling spent some time with the young man, to no pastoral effect, and on his way back to the rectory stopped at the Dolans. He was admitted by an elated Henry Dolan.

"Have you heard, Father?" he asked in the front hall. "It seems Maurice was just telling a story."

Catherine Adams was in the living room, seated on the couch with Vivian. Sheila Lynch, too, was there.

Although Catherine had confessed, she had been neither arrested nor indicted. This made her angry. "What more can I tell them? I rented the car. I told them Maurice had gone off God knows where and that I had arranged to meet Nate in Fox River. That's how I knew where to find him."

"You actually ran him down?" Vivian said in awed tones.

"I only meant to scare him."

"What had he done to you?"

Catherine now addressed herself to Father Dowling. "If that yo-yo of a prosecutor would read Nate's last novel, he would have it all."

"I read it," Vivian said. "Or tried to. Sheila passed it on to me. Did you read it all, Sheila?"

"Yes."

Catherine said, "Well, it's not just a story. Nate was fixated on the idea that he had to do something about his illegitimate child of long ago. He came back here determined to find the woman in the case. Nothing I said could deter him."

"I wonder if he found her," Vivian said.

"Of course he did."

Sheila's interest in what Catherine was saying intensified, but there was silence in the room.

Father Dowling tried desperately to change the subject. "I've just come from seeing Maurice," he said.

"Who was she?" Sheila asked.

"A woman married to a professor at Northwestern. I knew her all along. We were roommates when she had her baby at the Women's Care Center."

"Madeline!"

Seemingly unaware of what she had done, Catherine nodded. "So you already know her."

6

When the report from downstate came in, Phil Keegan was not in his office, so Cy went in search of Dr. Pippen. He found her in conference with Dennis Lubins, the coroner.

"Horvath," cried Lubins. "What's the news?"

The prospect of business filled the coroner with nervous anxiety. His political party had persuaded him to run for his office. He said yes against his better judgment, but his practice had not been flourishing, and he had been bewitched by the publicity attendant on the campaign. Somewhat to his astonishment, he had been voted in as coroner. He had little to recommend him for the job, and until he persuaded Pippen to become his assistant things had not gone well in the morgue.

"You remember that body found in the trunk of a car in the parking lot of the old depot?" Pippen asked.

"It was dead?"

Lubins laughed his nervous laugh. "Well,

I'll leave you young people to yourselves." Lubins was perhaps three years older than Cy. He skipped out of the room and was gone.

"You'd think you'd come courting," Pippen said.

"Too late for that." It was as close as he had ever come to admitting it was not just her mind that attracted him.

"The man died of a heart attack." She meant the body in the trunk.

"And then crawled in there to die?"

"The heart attack was probably caused by being locked in the trunk."

"Remember the hit-and-run on Dirksen Boulevard?"

"Of course. You have two people confessing to have done it."

"It can't have been either of them."

"How so?"

He showed her the report. The paint from the parking meter that had been knocked over by the vehicle involved did not match the sample Cy had scraped from the SUV rented by Catherine Adams. Pippen suggested they have coffee, but he countered with the offer to buy her a beer in the sports bar across the street.

"Oh, I love that place. All those games to ignore."

When they had crossed the street and were in the bar, Pippen asked for a nonalcoholic beer. Cy made a face.

"Don't you approve?"

"It's tampering with nature. I'm Catholic."

"So am I."

"You are!"

"Yes. I became one when I married my Ojibwa. Is it really against our religion?"

"Some instructions you must have received." He got her O'Doul's and a Guinness for himself, and they found a booth.

"The priest who instructed me didn't seem to know much."

"Then it couldn't have been Father Dowling."

"Let me see that report again." He gave it to her, and she got out her glasses.

"I didn't know you wore glasses."

"Only when I read."

"You didn't put them on before."

"That's why I wanted to see this again. It looks conclusive."

"Even if it was inconclusive those two are off the hook."

"Have they been charged?"

"You can't charge two people with the same crime when each claims to have acted alone. He was arraigned. Jacuzzi is going to feel like a fool, and try to make me look like one. He won't be far wrong."

"Maybe you should admit to the crime to clear everything up. What will happen to those two?"

"Nothing. Jacuzzi will probably threaten to bring charges against them for something or other, but it will only be a threat."

"So all's well that ends well."

"Somebody ran over that guy."

"Poor Cy. You really do hunger and thirst after justice, don't you?"

"Then I should be glad that Maurice Dolan and Catherine Adams get off scot-free."

"Aren't you?"

"She's kind of cute."

"I'll tell your wife."

It helped some to talk with Pippen about it, which had been the idea when he sought her out in the morgue, but after they parted, Cy went again to Phil Keegan's office. The captain was back, and Phil gave him the news.

"They must have used another vehicle."

"Well, it was another vehicle."

Phil shook his head in commiseration. One more unsolved crime to add to all the others. "Want a beer, Cy?"

He might have said he'd just had one, but he didn't. It was when they were approaching the bar that he remembered the vehicle Mark Lorenzo had left parked in front of the place when they went to see the Dolans. Before going on to the hospital, Cy had brought the professor back to the bar so he could pick it up.

All the while Cy was having a beer with Phil, his mind was working. Maybe the hit-and-run wouldn't end up unsolved after all. The thought made him more depressed than he had been. He liked Lorenzo. The more he thought of it, though, the less he found himself able to dismiss the possibility. If anyone had a motive to get rid of that author, Lorenzo did. The man was a threat to his wife and his family's happiness. Cy Horvath wouldn't have been Cy Horvath if he just put the idea out of his mind.

7

Mark Lorenzo had just returned from class when Cy Horvath came to his office. The detective took a seat and then told him about the negative report on the paint sample.

"Thank God!"

"That makes you happy?"

"When I read that she had confessed, I knew she couldn't have done it."

"How could you know that?"

"Because she was sitting in that same chair when it happened. I was her alibi. I have been trying to convince myself that I would just keep quiet."

"She was here?"

"Not for the first time. She was a former student of mine, years ago. I told you all that before. Before my marriage, she came to me with what she obviously thought was damning information about my intended bride."

"What did she want this time?"

"She came twice. The second time was to tell me how glad she was that the threat to

Madeline was gone, now that Nathaniel Fleck was dead. The way she put it made me think that she might have had something to do with his death, but she couldn't have. She was sitting right there when it happened."

"That was during the first visit?"

"When she came back, she seemed to want to take credit for easing the pressure on Madeline."

"The vehicle involved was an SUV."

"I know." Then he remembered the detective's diatribe about SUVs, prompted by the sight of Stephen's car. There was a long silence. "You want to see my son's car."

"It's just routine."

"Look, Horvath, if I was talking to Catherine Adams when the accident occurred . . ." He stopped. "Of course, you only have my word for that."

Horvath tipped his head to one side.

"I didn't want to be Catherine Adams's alibi, and I don't want her for mine." He stood. "Come on and take a look at Stephen's car."

There was no need to involve the son. The SUV was parked behind the residence hall in which Stephen lived. Horvath walked around it several times.

"There's no paint missing," the detective said.

"Is it the right color?"

"Close."

"Then take a sample, for God's sake."

"We might as well be sure."

"Right!"

"Lorenzo, I'm just doing my job."

"Then do it."

Horvath got out his knife and looked for a place where a little scratch wouldn't show.

"He keeps it in pretty good shape."

"He better. I'm paying for it."

Horvath scraped a little paint into a plastic bag, then put it in his pocket.

"You're going to get another negative result, Horvath."

"I hope so."

The detective walked back with Lorenzo. He had parked his car in a handicapped spot outside the faculty office building.

"What's your handicap?" Mark asked.

"Ten."

How could you be angry with a guy like Cy Horvath? Lorenzo punched the detective's arm and they parted.

Madeline was a different woman since she had met with Martha, despite the reaction of Mrs. Lynch when she showed up.

"Who can blame her, Mark? She must feel about me the way I felt about him."

"It's hardly the same."

"It would be to her."

"What's she like?"

"Mrs. Lynch?"

"Your daughter."

She looked at him quickly and then came and put her arms around him. The way he had said it seemed to drive a wedge between them, and he could have bitten his tongue as soon as he spoke. Now he held her wordlessly.

"Mark, it's all over now."

If anything is ever really over. Years ago, Madeline probably thought her troubles were all behind her when she had her baby and gave it up for adoption. It must have seemed like something that had never happened. That would have been her justification for not telling him. How he wished he had learned of it from her rather than from that vixen Catherine Adams. Madeline's anxiety had returned when first Dolan and then Catherine had claimed to have run down Nathaniel Fleck. She read the newspaper account carefully.

"You're not mentioned, Mad."

"Do you know the joke about the dyslexic mother against drunk driving who said she belonged to DDAM?"

When Madeline remembered a joke, she never felt very funny.

"You said it. It's all over."

She nodded, but she must have been thinking what he was. There was another joke that proved it.

"I'll never be my own worst enemy while Catherine is alive," Madeline said.

He didn't tell her about Horvath and the paint sample taken from Stephen's car.

8

Tuttle's bank account, presided over by Hazel, had been refreshed by recent events. Both Martin Sisk and Bernard Casey had paid what Tuttle regarded as the exorbitant fee Hazel had billed them for. Still, it was difficult to see Hazel as a blessing. When he had handed her the check Martin had scribbled in the car, she said, "I'll get this right into the bank. That rascal may try to stop payment."

Within days of the other bill's going out, payment was received from Bernard Casey as well.

"We're in clover, Tuttle."

Why didn't he feel elation? It wasn't just that, apart from the twenty dollars he had taken from Martin on his first visit, all the proceeds of his labors were in Hazel's control. The misgivings he had expressed to Martin before trying to deal directly with the Dolans had been almost sincere. He did feel tainted by helping to dredge up past events best left forgotten for the good of all concerned.

Hazel pooh-poohed such moralizing.

"You're a hired gun, Tuttle. Every lawyer is. You ought to know by now what legal ethics amounts to. Cover your rear."

He thought she had said "ear," so he cupped both his with his hands, waiting for her revelation about legal ethics. Hazel had worked for years in a firm that specialized in criminal law, the office joke being that the phrase was an oxymoron. Hazel had considered them all morons, defending rapists, defending killers, helping flown fathers escape responsibility for their families. It wasn't so much that she thought these things wrong as that they seemed a personal affront. It was too easy to imagine herself the victim in such cases. So she had come to Tuttle, first as a temporary and then, by a process he could never reconstruct, a permanent presence in his outer office, a tyrant with amorous tendencies. Tuttle was often thankful he could lock the door of his inner office when the tides of romance rose in Hazel's enormous breast.

"Something wrong with your ears?"

"Just covering them."

She found this witty. A warm look came over the face that would have done Mount Rushmore proud, and Tuttle skedaddled. Had his hope of diverting her attention to Martin Sisk been completely dashed?

"I feel like celebrating," Hazel crowed when she came back from the bank after depositing Casey's check.

"Don't let Martin turn it into a dutch treat. The man should always pay."

"Martin!"

"He seemed wistful the last time I talked with him."

"He always seems wistful. Imagine, a man his age watching the same movies over and over. And pictures of his late wife all over the place."

"Well, if you want to throw in the towel, Grace Weaver will walk him down the aisle."

"She the one who called me?"

"The same."

Hazel pondered this. Whether it was attraction to Martin Sisk or the prospect of losing him to a rival that decided her would have been difficult to say. "Well, I know the way to his heart."

"Please." He covered his ears.

She went on. "I'll buy him a movie, DVD, that's what he prefers. Any ideas?"

He left the door of his office open a crack and listened to her when she got on the phone to Martin. She had found the most wonderful movie for him. *Meet Me in St. Louis.* Apparently Martin was wild about old Judy Garland movies. Hazel seemed to have received a favorable response.

"My place or yours?"

She began to hum the title song. St. Louis in this case seemed to be Hazel's apartment. Tuttle closed his door.

Peanuts didn't know much about developments at headquarters, but Tetzel's lengthy accounts in the Trib kept Tuttle informed. First one person confessed to running down Nathaniel Fleck, then another. It seemed an obvious ploy to make both confessions useless. Peanuts did bring him the information about the report from downstate. That got the confessing couple off the hook. So who had run down the author?

Tuttle went to the courthouse and poured himself a cup of coffee in the pressroom. Tetzel's star was in the ascendant, and he was enjoying his moment. He even returned Tuttle's greeting.

"So who ran the man down?" Tuttle asked.

For answer, Tetzel printed out a copy of the story he had just sent to his paper. In it he opined that we are often led astray by our insistence that events are part of a causal theory. Something happens, somebody must have caused it. But often the somebody did not intend what the something.

Tuttle looked up from the page. "Are they going to print this?"

It turned out that Tetzel had printed out his initial ruminations before writing his story. Soon he put a copy of that into Tuttle's hands.

When Nathaniel Fleck was struck by a car that jumped the curb on Dirksen Boulevard, sending the author through a window and to his death, it was an accident pure and simple, police investigation indicates. The motorist who fled the scene very likely did not know that his temporary loss of control of his vehicle had resulted in the death of the renowned author.

The story cascaded from that beginning paragraph. In midstory, good citizen Tetzel urged the motorist to identify himself and clear the air once and for all. He, or she, need fear no charge more grievous than leaving the scene of an accident.

Tuttle left the pressroom and the courthouse. Across the street a preoccupied Cy Horvath emerged from the sports bar. Tuttle watched him head for the police garage. He was behind the wheel of his car when Cy emerged, and he followed him.

When they reached the Northwestern campus, Tuttle waited for Cy to get out of the car, which he had parked in a handicapped spot. Horvath entered the building, and a minute later Tuttle followed.

A thin girl with overbite and glasses halfway down her nose regarded him. "Yes?"

"My brother just came in here. A big fellow —"

She was already nodding. "He's with Professor Lorenzo."

He thanked her and went out to his car. Lorenzo. He would be the husband of the Madeline Lorenzo Tuttle had located for both Bernard Casey and the Dolans, via Martin Sisk. Again Tuttle felt a faint regret for what he had done. The Dolans, inhospitable as they had proved to be, were parents of a daughter who they had taken in as a child born out of wedlock, a noble deed in Tuttle's book. And the young mother must have fought off suggestions that she abort her baby. Another noble choice. For those past events to rise to the surface now threatened the lives of both the adopting parents, the Lynches, and Madeline Lorenzo and her husband. A philosopher. He wondered what grade Lorenzo would have given Tetzel's speculative reflections. Cy's visit suggested that the story was otherwise than

Tetzel thought and that Lorenzo was somehow involved.

When the two men emerged and began to
walk across campus, Tuttle followed. How
unaware the watched are that they are being
watched. It was a thought worthy of Tetzel.
Nonetheless, Tuttle looked over his
shoulder, lest the follower be followed. Of
course there was no one behind him.

Lorenzo led Cy to a parking lot, where
they examined a vehicle. An SUV! Cy
walked around the vehicle inspecting it and
then began to scrape some paint from an
area behind the huge spare mounted on the
back. Aha. Soon the two men headed back
the way they had come. Tuttle's pulse was
racing. If Lorenzo had now become the object of Cy's investigation, he would need
legal representation. Tuttle began to re-
hearse the approach he would make when
he confronted the philosopher.

But excitement drained from him as he
followed Cy and the professor, and his earlier distaste returned. It helped, perhaps,
that he had already profited sufficiently
from Martha Lynch's desire to find her real
mother. Somewhere his sainted father
seemed to be suggesting that he stay out of it
now that he was out of it. Tuttle was not
given to abstract generalization. When he

thought of the Lorenzos and Lynches it was on analogy with the warm household in which he had been raised on the South Side. The family is sacred. By the time he slipped behind the wheel of his car, Tuttle had decided against ambulance chasing, at least for the nonce.

Cy was standing with the professor at the door of the building. What would the detective say if he knew he had been observed? Satisfaction with his own cunning was sufficient reward for this excursion.

Lorenzo punched Cy's arm, and Cy got into his car. He backed up, coming right at Tuttle. His back bumper struck Tuttle's front bumper, jolting his ancient car.

Cy stuck his head out the window. "Tuttle? You can follow me back, too. I wouldn't want you to get lost."

When Cy pulled away, there was a metallic complaint from Tuttle's car. He put it in gear and followed Horvath back to Fox River. From time to time, he looked in his rearview mirror, but no one was following him.

9

The marriage of Martha Lynch and Bernard Casey was the social event of the year at St. Hilary's. There were three bridesmaids — one rather elderly, Willa — and, complementing them, three Notre Dame classmates of Casey's. The bride, of course, was beautiful, and she and the groom looked like the ideal little statuettes atop their wedding cake. Father Dowling said the nuptial Mass and witnessed the vows of the young couple. In the front pews on the groom's side of the aisle was a great complement of Caseys, headed by Bernard's parents, and opposite them were the Lynches, joined in the front pew by Henry and Vivian Dolan, Maurice, and his perhaps fiancée, Catherine Adams, a lovely little hat atop her cropped head. Two pews behind the family was the imposing figure of Amos Cadbury. Of course, Catherine Adams did not come forward at communion time, nor as it happened did George Lynch. In a back pew a woman whose mantilla not only covered her hair but put her face in shadows followed the ceremony with tears in her eyes. She might have been a sister of the bride. She, too, remained in her pew while communion was being distributed.

Afterward, everyone adjourned to the erstwhile school, which had been transformed for the reception. In one corner of the former gym, a quartet played background music before the guests sat down to partake of the veritable banquet the Lynches had provided.

Marie Murkin was in seventh heaven and was willing to share responsibility for the occasion with Edna Hospers, director of the senior center. In truth, neither woman had done a thing; all preparations were made by people sent in by the Lynches. Father Dowling circulated, feeling somewhat superfluous now that his role had been played.

"He broke his fast," Marie whispered in his ear. "Dr. Lynch. Mrs. Lynch told me."

"Why would she have done that?"

"I have no idea. Of course I noticed he hadn't taken communion and asked if he was non-Catholic."

This was not the time or place to scold Marie for her unpardonable behavior. She hurried away from his expression, and he resolved to read the riot act to her later in the rectory. Imagine, putting such questions to the mother of the bride. But he knew his anger would cool and he would not speak sharply to Marie. When he wasn't wondering what he would do with her, he wondered what he would do without her.

Eventually, everyone was seated, the bride and groom at a raised table, flanked by their parents, the others at the twenty or more tables arranged around the room, relatives and friends, luminaries of the legal and medical professions. Father Dowling took the microphone and said the grace. Now he could slip away without offense. Indeed, without being noticed. Marie and Edna were seated at a table featuring frequent visitors to the senior center. Before he reached the door, there was the sound of silverware striking glass, an insistent sound. The bride and groom kissed to great applause. Father Dowling left and soon was settled in his study with his pipe lit.

Not so long ago, Henry Dolan had spoken to him in this room of the anxiety created in his family by his granddaughter's intention to discover her birth mother. Well, Martha's wish had been fulfilled, and the Lynches and Dolans were intact. Madeline Lorenzo's attendance at the wedding had been self-effacing, and of course she had not come to the reception. Her family, too, had apparently been unaffected by Martha's desire.

The doorbell rang, and for a moment Father Dowling resented the disruption of his solitude, but he rose and went to the door. Amos Cadbury stood there.

"I saw you leave, Father, and thought I might stop by."

"Wonderful, Amos. Come in, come in."

Amos had had a glass of champagne at the reception before the food was served. He accepted Father Dowling's offer of some Irish whiskey.

"Powers," he said, impressed.

"I thought Phil Keegan might like it, but he prefers beer."

"It is the best of the best."

"Oh, I had my share, Amos."

The venerable lawyer nodded. No need to expatiate on that. He lit a cigar and sipped his Powers, a picture of contentment. "I could not help thinking what possible disasters the Lynches have been spared."

"And the Lorenzos."

"Of course."

"She was there, Martha's mother."

"Was she?"

"There, but unobserved."

"That, of course, was as it should be. Doubtless Martha knew she was present."

Amos frowned. "It is Maurice Dolan's behavior I find irksome. More than irksome. Whatever the nadir into which the law has fallen, I hate to see it made a mockery of. Imagine, the two of them confessing to a crime they could not have committed."

"Each thought the other had."

"Perhaps. Until their vehicle was ruled out, I was of the school that held they had hit on a way to get away with murder by confessing to it."

Father Dowling was of the school that believed Maurice had performed an altruistic act, meant to shield Catherine Adams. That she had replied in kind made him think more highly of her. Of course, he could understand Amos's professional resentment.

"May the past be the past at last," Amos said.

Father Dowling lifted his coffee mug in response to Amos's raised glass.

"Of course, there is still the unexplained death of Nathaniel Fleck."

"The local paper has decided it was simply an accident."

"But has Cy Horvath?"

Amos smiled. "God help that driver if Cy still has anything to go on."

Father Dowling had heard from Phil Keegan about the negative results of testing the paint sample taken from young Lorenzo's SUV. It seemed that Cy's last suspicion had proved unfounded.

"I think he was glad about it," Phil said. "Of course, with Cy you're never sure. He is not a demonstrative man."

It was difficult not to share Amos's wish that the past be the past at last.

10

On the following Wednesday, the staff and volunteers of the Women's Care Center came to the noon Mass at St. Hilary's, and afterward there was a luncheon in the gym, utilizing the tables rented by the Lynches, which were still in place. The group filled five tables. Father Dowling was impressed and remarked on it to Louise, the director of the center.

"And this is not everyone, Father. Not all the volunteers, certainly. For example, Dr. Lynch could not come."

"Dr. Lynch."

"Such a wonderful man. He gives us several hours a week."

"Counseling?"

"Yes. The fact that he is a doctor makes him very effective."

"I should imagine."

"And now he has given us a vehicle as well."

"He has."

Louise lowered her voice. "Not an ideal one for our purposes. It is one of these huge tanklike things. Not easy for expectant mothers to get in and out of."

"That was very generous of him."

"Would you like to see it? I drove it here."

The SUV was in the parking lot next to the school. Father Dowling circled it, making appropriate remarks. The only flaw was a crease in the right front fender, with some missing paint.

"Dr. Lynch said he would pay for that if we made arrangements."

They went back inside. Father Dowling noticed a novel protruding from the bag that hung from Louise's shoulder. It was a copy of *The Long Good-bye.*

"Are you enjoying it?"

"I hate it."

"So why are you reading it? It isn't Lent."

Again she dropped her voice. "The author came by the center one day. He wanted the identity of one of our mothers. From years ago, before I came to the center. Of course I told him nothing."

"Nathaniel Fleck visited the Women's Care Center?"

"Isn't that a strange name?"

"Do you remember who he was looking for?"

"I wouldn't listen. I tried to stop him saying anything, but he was most persistent.

372

I think he must have been that child's father. Well, Dr. Lynch came to the rescue."

He listened to her describe the firm way in which Lynch had followed the man into the parking lot, then away, gone off with him somewhere.

"He never came back?"

"Oh, no."

Father Dowling looked at Louise. Hadn't she read of Fleck's death on Dirksen Boulevard? But surely she would have made the connection with her unwanted visitor if she had. Doubtless it is a small percentage of people who are aware of or interested in what is regarded as the news of the day. Yet Louise was trying to read Fleck's novel. It might have seemed inevitable that she must learn that Fleck had not only been a visitor at the center and the author of the novel but that he had been killed on Dirksen Boulevard when an SUV drove onto the sidewalk to hit him.

The following day, Marie opened the door to George Lynch, and as she led him to the pastor, she gushed about how wonderful the wedding had been. Then he was in the doorway. Father Dowling rose to greet him and got him seated, and Marie went merrily away.

"I've come to thank you for my daughter's wedding, Father. Everything was as we wished."

"And as you arranged, George. I had little to do with it."

"It must have put you to extra expense. Please let me cover that."

"I am as likely to bill the Women's Care Center for the Mass and lunch they had here yesterday."

"Surely I can make a donation to the parish."

Father Dowling thought about it. "If there is something Edna Hospers should need at the senior center . . ."

"I'll ask. Vivian and Henry are great fans. Perhaps we could combine on something or other."

"Perhaps. Louise told me that you do volunteer work at the center."

George looked beyond Father Dowling and then met his eyes. "My wife and I owe everything to that place. It is thanks to the center that we got Martha."

"I was told that Martha's father had come there, making inquiries."

George said nothing, but what he was thinking registered in his eyes.

"She also showed me the SUV you donated to them."

There are moments so pregnant with possibilities that no one can predict what will emerge from them. This was one. Father Dowling did not need to be more explicit to let George Lynch realize what he had discovered. The foster father who would do anything for his adopted daughter had meant it. Only after a long silence did he speak.

"How can I protect Martha from this?"

"The first thing you should do is talk to Cy Horvath."

George Lynch nodded.

"Perhaps that is the second thing."

"And what is the first?"

"Confessing what you have done to God and asking his forgiveness."

"How can even he forgive me?"

Father Dowling got out a stole and put it on. He was not an advocate of hustling people to the sacraments, only of making them easily available.

"Should I kneel, Father?"

"That isn't necessary."

And so it was that Father Dowling as a stand-in for the Almighty first heard George Lynch's story. Of course, it was told to him in a different vein than it was afterward to the police. The great obstacle for George was that he could not say he wished he had not done what he had done. It would have been Pickwickian to ask him to promise never to do again what he had done. Nathaniel Fleck had been a unique case. Eventually, George acknowledged that he was sorry he was not sorry, and Father Dowling gave him absolution, praying down pardon and peace on a soul that had loved not wisely but too well.

About the Author

Ralph McInerny is the author of more than thirty books, including a mystery series set at the University of Notre Dame, where he has taught for more than forty years and directs the Jacques Maritain Center. He has been awarded the Bouchercon Lifetime Achievement Award and is a member of the President's Committee on the Arts and Humanities. He lives in South Bend, Indiana.